"You're

That...was not what she'd expected to come out of his mouth. "I don't...I don't understand. As of three hours ago, I was convinced I was being fired. What could have changed?"

For the first time, Branch met her gaze without so much as a wince from the sound of her voice. And waited for her to connect the dots.

"You convinced him to keep me." She braced herself for the argument, but it never came. "Why would you do that? You can't stand me."

Branch stared down at her. Not intimidating. Just... there. Like he would sign up to fight all of her battles if he could, even the ones she'd kept to herself. "The Grotto at six." He didn't wait for her to answer as he practically lunged for the door. "Don't be late."

Lila couldn't help but scramble after him. "Why? What's at six?"

Branch pulled up short of crossing the threshold back out into the gusty darkness and locked his gaze on her. "We start tracking the killer."

DISAPPEARANCE AT ANGEL'S LANDING

NICHOLE SEVERN

INTRIGUE

If you purchased this book without a cover you should be aware that this book is stolen property. It was reported as "unsold and destroyed" to the publisher, and neither the author nor the publisher has received any payment for this "stripped book."

To my husband:
for managing to keep me from going insane
during COVID-19 quarantine so I could write this book.

ISBN-13: 978-1-335-69021-0

Disappearance at Angel's Landing

Copyright © 2025 by Natascha Jaffa

All rights reserved. No part of this book may be used or reproduced in any manner whatsoever without written permission.

Without limiting the author's and publisher's exclusive rights, any unauthorized use of this publication to train generative artificial intelligence (AI) technologies is expressly prohibited.

This is a work of fiction. Names, characters, places and incidents are either the product of the author's imagination or are used fictitiously. Any resemblance to actual persons, living or dead, businesses, companies, events or locales is entirely coincidental.

For questions and comments about the quality of this book, please contact us at CustomerService@Harlequin.com.

TM and ® are trademarks of Harlequin Enterprises ULC.

 Harlequin Enterprises ULC
22 Adelaide St. West, 41st Floor
Toronto, Ontario M5H 4E3, Canada
www.Harlequin.com

Printed in Lithuania

Nichole Severn writes explosive romantic suspense with strong heroines, heroes who dare challenge them and a hell of a lot of guns. She resides with her very supportive and patient husband, as well as her demon spawn, in Utah. When she's not writing, she's constantly injuring herself running, rock climbing, practicing yoga and snowboarding. She loves hearing from readers through her website, www.nicholesevern.com, and on Facebook at nicholesevern.

Books by Nichole Severn

Harlequin Intrigue

Red Rock Murders

Manhunt in the Narrows
Disappearance at Angel's Landing

New Mexico Guard Dogs

K-9 Security
K-9 Detection
K-9 Shield
K-9 Guardians
K-9 Confidential
K-9 Justice

Defenders of Battle Mountain

Grave Danger
Dead Giveaway
Dead on Arrival
Presumed Dead
Over Her Dead Body
Dead Again

Visit the Author Profile page at Harlequin.com.

CAST OF CHARACTERS

Lila Jordan — She loathes the nickname "Ranger Barbie," but will happily let people think what they want as long as they don't look too close. As an overly optimistic search and rescue ranger, Lila will do anything to assist in the recovery of a missing hiker last seen on Angel's Landing. Even if it means partnering up with a man who can't stand her.

Branch Thompson — This park service ranger takes his job of keeping park visitors alive seriously. Nothing and no one will get in the way of doing his job. Until he's forced to partner with a ridiculously happy search and rescue ranger who tests his limits at every turn with her forked tongue and death threats.

Sarah Lantos — Originally believed to be an accident victim on the perilous five-thousand-foot cliffside hike of Angel's Landing, Sarah isn't everything she seems…

Zion National Park — Two hundred and thirty-two square miles of trails, red rock and danger waiting to happen.

Chapter One

"Quick. Here come one of the pine pigs."

That was a new one.

National Park Ranger Lila Jordan pasted on a practiced smile as she hauled herself up the steep first section of Angel's Landing, the 5,900-ft near-vertical crown jewel that looked out over the expanse of Zion National Park. The name came from some Methodist minister in the 1900s who'd commented that only an angel could land up here and had somehow stuck.

This was the most popular hike in the park for those looking for untamed adventure and that classic photo op, but Angel's Landing had also taken a number of lives over the years. Which was why Lila's legs were currently burning despite years of hiking this particular trail to catch up to two yahoos. While safety was left to hikers—like the two men trying to avoid eye contact ahead of her, probably due to the fact they'd sneaked onto the trail without applying for a permit—she couldn't really let them die out here out of stupidity. Unfortunately for the benefit of mankind. "Morning, gentlemen. Can you please show me your permits and ID?"

"Uh, yeah." The hiker on her left really wasn't anything to write home about with his bland features, bland brown hair and bland ability to lie his way out of a hole. He patted his pants pockets, then his flannel shirt in a vain attempt to buy himself some time. "I've got it here somewhere."

Lila angled her gaze to the second hiker decked out in nearly every piece of equipment the little town outside of Zion sold. Brand-new boots with a slight film of red dust, a lightweight jacket with the tag still hanging out the back and a backpack most likely stuffed with days' worth of food for a five-mile hike. "How about you? You got a permit?"

His smile flashed wide. All right. Turning on the charm straight away. That had to be a record in her book. "Well, uh. You see, there was a mix-up with the lottery. I got the email we were approved, but I accidentally deleted it."

Right. Anyone applying for a permit on Angel's Landing had to enter a daily drawn lottery so rangers could keep track of how many hikers—and who—were out on the trail. The park had implemented the pilot program during the COVID-19 pandemic but kept it to ensure all hikers made it off the trail in one piece. She couldn't promise these two would.

Lila kept her own smile in place, showcasing perfectly straight white teeth guaranteed to blind given the right angle of the sun. She unhitched her radio from her belt, catching the clip on one of the hot pink jeweled studs she'd hot glued to the faux leather because life was too short to die in a drab gray and tan uniform. It didn't matter how many times the district ranger wrote her up for insubordination. "That's not a problem. We have record of everyone who was approved for a permit today. I just need to see your IDs and confirm your names with rangers on the ground."

The smile slipped, but this guy wasn't going to just

admit he and his friend had broken the rules to get on the trail. Or take her seriously.

She got that a lot. Mostly from men just like him. The ones who only saw her blond hair tucked back into a curled ponytail under her Stetson, the soft pink lip gloss she didn't go anywhere without and the floral pink kerchief tied at her neck.

His head-to-toe leer turned her stomach. "You sure you're a ranger? Way I see it, you're way too pretty to hide out here in the park all day."

"Awww. Aren't you sweet?" She added a rise in her voice on that last word, dipping one leg to shift her weight with a little bit of Southern charm despite the fact she'd come from the middle of nowhere Utah. A little bounce meant to tell prey she was too bashful to take a compliment. It was one of the many weapons in her arsenal to stop anyone from looking past the Ranger Barbie armor.

That was what all the other rangers here in the park called her. In whispers and conversations that stopped short of her approach. In the roll of their eyes and placating words when she volunteered for the most dangerous rescue assignments. She had the same training as they did, with a record number of rescues, yet her penchant for pretty things and pink accessories had somehow put her at the bottom of the list. Like getting picked last in kickball in elementary school.

The only one who let her join in on the ranger reindeer games was her roommate Sayles, and that traitor spent more time with her FBI agent boyfriend than late nights watching crappy romantic comedies with Lila these days.

"Fortunately for you, my looks have nothing to do with my ability to ensure neither of you die on this trail. So you can show me your permits with today's date and your IDs, or I can have you escorted off the trail."

Shock turned the silence between them into something physical. If their eyes could bug out anymore, they'd be rolling down the trail.

"What a bitch." The first hiker took a step toward her, as if she was nothing but a cute yippy dog blocking their ascent to Scout Lookout.

"But you still think I'm pretty, right?" Lila let that sweet smile light up her face as she replaced her radio and unclipped her Taser. Pressing the power button, she let it charge for a few seconds. "Who wants to go first?"

An hour later, Lila handed over both hikers to the law enforcement rangers stationed out of the park headquarters near the Zion National Park museum. They'd pay a fine with a warning not to attempt the trail without a permit again. Wouldn't stop them. No matter how many hikers she dragged off Angel's Landing, another dozen slipped her notice and made it all that much harder for those who followed the rules.

Her radio crackled from her belt before a voice that curdled her insides cleared over the channel. "Jordan, come in."

A deep sigh escaped before she could control it. Here she thought she could lose herself on the trail for a couple hours and avoid any semblance of Rick Risner. Yep, that was his real name, though she and the other rangers preferred to call him by his formal title. Pinheaded F—

"Yeah, boss?"

Risner kept her in suspense for close to a minute before responding. It was a tool he kept in his own arsenal to piss off every man, woman and child who stepped into this park. Including his subordinates, which he liked to remind her was every ranger in a two-hundred-and-thirty-mile radius. "We've got a possible missing hiker on Angel's Landing. Name is Sarah Lantos. Made her start time at six this morning, hasn't been spotted since. Dark hair, about five foot six, license puts her at thirty-nine years old."

Lila checked her smartwatch. It was close to noon with the sun blazing overhead and working to undo all that care she'd put into her hair this morning. Even the slowest hikers made it back to the base of the hike—the Grotto—in around four hours with scenic interludes and photography opportunities along the way.

Six hours. Was the hiker injured? Had she been traveling with anyone else? Could she have decided to stay at the peak longer than most? Maybe the woman had forgotten to check in with the permit office or managed to avoid a ranger on her descent. Except none of those reasons eased the acid lodged in her throat. Lila bent to collect the jewel that fell from her belt and pinched the push-to-talk button on the radio. "I'm headed back up now."

"Update me in an hour." No *thanks, Lila* or *be careful, Lila*. Actually, she wasn't even sure Risner knew her first name. He'd only called her Jordan for the past two years since she signed on with the National Park Service. Last named. Unimportant, not worth getting to know as a person. Merely a tool. It was the same for the other female rangers on staff, but he certainly made an effort with everyone else, i.e., the men. A true pine pig.

Oooh, she'd have to tell Sayles about the new nickname tonight.

The hot pink jewel reflected back at her in the center of her palm. There wasn't time to fix it now. She'd have to wait until her shift ended. She tucked the good little soldier into her slacks pocket. She hadn't moved out here to the middle of nowhere with a lot of luxuries, but she'd made damn sure her hot glue gun and bedazzling kit made the cut.

Lila grabbed two bottles of water from the park headquarters' break room along with a couple of protein bars for the trek back to Angel's Landing. Breakfast of champions…four hours too late. Okay, so she probably should eat more vegetables, but convenience was the name of the game.

Summer in Zion had hit full force, and the heat never let her forget it. Storms broke up the days, but this was the busiest time of year in the park. Kids were out of school and driving their parents crazy. What better way than to force them up a mountain—or three—to burn off some of that energy? No time for home-cooked meals in these parts.

Smooth red rock resembling melted taffy acted as stairs as she ascended the first section of the trail. Hikers could climb the first two and a half miles of the West Rim Trail without a permit. It was the second half of the overly popular, adrenaline-inducing, nothing-but-chains-to-hold-onto, 6000-foot drop Angel's Landing was known for. There were days a line of people started at the base and grouped at the end.

Thankfully, she could move at her own pace through Walter's Wiggles—a series of twenty-one switchbacks leading to Scout Lookout—without pushing anyone off the side of the cliff today. Rock turned to sand under her boots and added an additional layer of burn. She'd always been in shape, going from yoga to biking to marathon training and rock climbing over the years when she needed a change, but hiking would be the one to kill her in the end.

Mountains surged upward from every angle as she navigated the incessant rise of rough terrain. Chains signaled the beginning of the most difficult portion of the trail, the one leading straight to eighteen people's deaths in the past fifty years. Even as a ranger, she wasn't invincible. Or stupid. She used the chains to propel her up the incline, the metal biting into her palm.

Spots of winter white still clung to north-facing peaks, adding a bite to the air. Jagged surges in rock threatened every step, but she'd hiked this trail more times than she could count. What most considered a once-in-a-lifetime adventure had become part of her daily routine. Sometimes two to three times a day. Barren pines and scrub brush peppered the rock face along the final ascent to the top.

No sign of Sarah Lantos. Though there'd been a couple lookalikes she'd stopped to ask for ID, Lila couldn't dislodge the dread pooling at the base of her spine as she summited the peak. A few hikers snapped photos, a couple getting too close to the chains following the edge of the cliff face and providing unobstructed views of the canyon below.

Sarah Lantos wouldn't have just disappeared off the trail. Allowing herself to feel the fear of falling and forcing herself to do it anyway, Lila stretched out over the near-nonexistent barrier between her and certain death. And caught a hint of bright yellow six thousand feet below.

Her chest squeezed—too hard—as she grabbed for her radio. Another jewel abandoned ship, following the projection of the body below. "Risner, I think I found Sarah Lantos."

Chapter Two

People were morons.

Ranger Branch Thompson shoved through the ring of park visitors inching closer to the body. Always pushing to get a better look. As if the woman at the bottom of the cliff was some kind of tick in their to-do list during their national park tour. "Vultures."

Law enforcement rangers were already at work to secure a perimeter around the fallen hiker, but national parks weren't equipped like a regular police force. While rangers followed similar protocols during death investigations, they didn't have crime scene tape, a forensic unit or the manpower to ensure the area around the body wasn't compromised. That was where he came in.

Branch caught sight of a bright yellow jacket—unmoving—in the center of the controlled chaos. Risner, the district ranger, hadn't given him a lot of information on the hiker who'd taken a flying leap off Angel's Landing when he'd ordered Branch to help with crowd control. But Branch noted long red hair and thin fingers splayed out to the hiker's side. Female, from the look of it.

Extending his arms out to either side, he forced the crowd back a couple feet, his expression more than ready to shut down questions. Facing off with two dozen onlookers grated his nerves raw. Why he'd chosen to interact with the public all day in a too-hot box surrounded by things that could eat and kill him, he'd never know. Felt right at the time, he guessed.

And now the park had a death on its hands. Nothing short of a miracle would convince the superintendent to close it. With over five million visitors a year—charged a minimum of thirty-five dollars a vehicle—Zion National Park was one of the most sought-after attractions in the west. The last time the National Park Service had been asked to evacuate Zion had been at the FBI's request during a violent manhunt that ended with an agent and one of Branch's fellow rangers almost dying in the process.

Park Service members had all signed on to protect the park from the people and the people from the park. They knew what they were getting themselves into. Knew the risks. But a hiker who hadn't followed personal safety suggestions before attacking the tallest and steepest trail in the park? This was just another day in Branch's book.

The line of bystanders closed in with their phones and cameras at the ready, questions and whispers and theories flying back and forth. Group mentality tended to do that. It took morality out of the equation. While having a hiker take a dive off one of the country's most dangerous trails wasn't an every day occurrence, Branch wasn't going to give anyone a shot at disgracing the body. "No photos. Step back. I won't tell you a second time."

Pressure built as eyes turned toward him him. Amid the crowd, he noted a flash of pink. A burn that had nothing to do with unobstructed sun bearing down on him lit up under his skin. Heaven help them all if Risner had called her in to help with this mess.

Lila Jordan, or more accurate, the bane of his existence.

The Barbie-like ranger bypassed the crowd and cut straight toward him, a smile plastered on her face. Shiny blond hair had been sleeked back into a ponytail beneath her Stetson, but she'd spent time curling the ends for added bounce. As always. No other female ranger in this park went so far as to wear makeup or keep up her hot pink manicure. And did she just wave at him? "Hi, Branch. Great job on crowd control!"

A growl resonated in his chest as he tracked her to the inner circle of rangers assessing the body. What the hell had Risner been thinking, hiring a woman who accessorized her uniform like Cupid threw up after an all-night Valentines Day binge?

The district ranger himself followed close on Lila's heels without so much as throwing Branch a glance, his eyes glued to her backside. Risner hadn't been thinking with the head above his belt, that was for sure, despite the thick gold band on his ring finger.

Acid curdled in Branch's stomach at the thought of the district ranger leering at Lila or any of the other female rangers in the service. While Branch would do anything to get out of a shift with Ranger Barbie—her enthusiasm and nonstop talking produced some of the most vicious migraines in existence—she didn't deserve her boss's lewd attention.

Though he doubted Lila hadn't used it to her advantage once or twice. Women like her were used to getting what they wanted through any means necessary, just like his ex-wife, with no concern for the trail of bodies in their wake. Lila had probably manipulated Risner into allowing her to join this investigation with a few bats of those long eyelashes and glossed lips. He wouldn't put it past her. Couldn't fault her, either, considering Risner's penchant for overlooking female rangers for the high-priority assignments. Zion didn't have more than a handful, but they were as crucial to running this place and keeping visitors alive as their male counterparts.

The burn beneath his skin was on the verge of consuming him at the thought of Lila using her beauty to influence Risner. She probably gave that son of a bitch the same smile she'd flashed him.

Nope. Didn't matter. Wasn't his business.

"Someone fell?" A visitor craned her head over Branch's shoulder to get a better look at the scene, a feat in and of itself. Her cracked lips told him she hadn't drunk enough water in these temperatures. If she didn't rectify that soon, he'd have to haul her out of here when she collapsed from dehydration.

Branch set his unimpressed gaze on her, watchful of any others who might think to break the line he'd created to give rangers the space they needed. "I'm not at liberty to say."

Still craning to see around his large frame, the visitor hiked onto her tiptoes, swaying toward him. She slapped her hand against his arm to catch herself. "Do you know who she was?"

"What part of *I'm not at liberty to say* didn't you understand?" He shucked her hand from his arm.

"Aren't you rangers supposed to be nice?" She landed back on her feet, sweat beading her upper lip. "My taxes pay your salary. The least you could do is pretend you know something about customer service."

"I'll keep that in mind." Branch forced himself to refocus on his job, but Ranger Barbie's incessant high-pitched drone proved too much to ignore. It probably deafened dogs.

He hadn't come up with Lila's nickname. Actually, he

wasn't sure where he'd heard it the first time, but the shoe fit with her pink socks, pink jewels decorating her belt, the pink nail polish and the pink bandana tied at her neck. He'd never met someone so disrespectful of the uniform.

He turned back to the hiker. "Drink something before I get called to come collect you off the trails."

Her shock only lasted a second. "You—"

"Branch, want to give us a hand?" Risner's question was more of a command.

It pissed Branch the hell off. He'd been doing just fine all the way over here, as far from Lila as he could get. Though his ears would argue it wasn't far enough. "Any of you move, and I'll have you banned from the park for life." Leaving his post, Branch closed the distance between him and the small ring of rangers staring down at the remains.

The near-6000-foot drop hadn't been kind. The hiker's bright yellow jacket contained most of the mess, but unmistakable brain matter splayed out in a burst of red and pink against the dirt. A hand had survived, at an odd angle, but it was there.

Risner pointed at the body. "The medical examiner is ready to turn her over to search her front pockets. Hopefully get a positive ID. Grab a side and help me lift her."

"How?" Branch's stomach revolted at the idea of… pieces slipping through his fingers, but he wouldn't lose his breakfast. Not here and sure as hell not in front of anyone. Weakness would only cost him.

"You could imagine it's a sensory bin." Lila set brilliant blue eyes on him, the color of which could shift from stormy to clear in a matter of seconds depending on her mood. Right now, they were somewhere in the middle. Most likely due to the fact a dead hiker had interrupted her afternoon of chasing unicorns and rainbows or whatever the hell she did out here. "Have you ever played with a container of those water beads you can squish between your fingers?"

Branch swallowed back a rush of bile. Did she seriously just compare a dead person to squishing a water bead? Leveling Ranger Barbie with every ounce of hatred in his bones, he let his revulsion for everything she stood for bleed into his expression.

His obvious dislike didn't deter her. "What about slime? Have you ever played with slime? I have some in my trailer. I buy it from a seventeen-year-old named Melissa who makes over three hundred different kinds right from her bedroom. She's an internet sensation. She puts all different kinds of things in it, like cotton candy scent, crunchy glue, sprinkles and any color you can imagine. And she does ASMR videos, especially when she uses foam beads. I can send you her socials if you—"

"Let's get this over with."

Ranger Barbie's smile slipped slightly, but within a second, it was right back in place.

Branch stepped up to the body. Definitely not thinking about the kind of noises a broken body trapped in a yellow jacket might make once they got their hands on her.

He took the fallen hiker's right side while Lila took the left, putting them opposite each other. A hint of her perfume—one he couldn't seem to stop himself from inhaling—tickled the back of his throat. Something ambery and feminine. Like a dual personality. Jekyll and Hyde. Who in their right mind wore perfume in over a hundred-degree heat in the middle of the desert?

Risner took control of the hiker's shoulders, his feet

spread wide to avoid the carnage around him. "One. Two. Three." Risner moved first.

They worked as one, slowly turning the remains, and set the hiker on her back. The body had stiffened some. Rigor mortis was setting in. Not at all like squishing water beads or playing with slime.

Lila dusted her hands, that irritating smile back in place with an exaggerated shoulder shrug. "Well, that wasn't so bad. Not as gooey as I thought it would be. Great job, team—"

"Can you shut up and show some respect for once?" The words snapped out of Branch's mouth before he had a chance to think it through.

The instant flash in her gaze told him he'd at least accomplished breaking through her cheerfulness. Lila cocked her head to one side, all signs of that Ranger Barbie smile buried. "Can you imagine what it will feel like when I open a Nature Valley granola bar on your bed?"

Branch fought against a resulting shiver. He could feel the crumbs already.

"Jordan, knock it off." Risner hiked his chin toward the medical examiner. "Search her pockets. We need a positive ID to inform the family of the accident."

Jordan? Since when did Risner address rangers by their last names?

"This wasn't an accident." Lila held Branch's gaze, almost daring him to interrupt her again. Or planning his murder. Branch couldn't be sure. Crouching beside the body, she pointed to a dark pattern of blood around a hole in the hiker's jacket. She unzipped the yellow abomination, revealing a deeper laceration. A stab wound. She glared at Branch before standing. "Sarah Lantos was murdered."

Chapter Three

She couldn't stop her hands from shaking.

Lila tried to breathe through her mouth as she, Branch and Risner transferred the remains to a black body bag. The squelching in her hands was nothing like a sensory bin or playing with slime. Sarah Lantos's body had basically exploded on impact but couldn't escape the confines of her clothing, so putting a pretty label on the squishiness of bone and sinew didn't do much to ease the nausea in Lila's stomach.

But she wasn't going to let it show. She wasn't about to lose the banana she'd forced down her throat an hour ago. Not here and definitely not in front of Branch Thompson.

His name alone threatened to notch her body temperature a couple of degrees higher. The man had been made of sex appeal. If the National Park Service put together a yearbook of their rangers, Branch Thompson would easily win every Best category: eyes, smile, laugh, athleticism. He had it all.

Sigh. That strong jaw could slice her hand open if she wasn't careful, though she hadn't ever gotten the opportunity. He'd made sure of that.

With shorn hair, an abundance of muscle and a partially hidden spider tattoo stretching from the left side of his collar, he looked as though he'd stepped off the cover of a military magazine. She couldn't be sure if he'd served. Actually, she didn't know a whole lot about him other than he'd transferred from another park earlier in the year. Okay. Four months, two weeks and six days ago. But she wasn't counting.

Branch tended to keep to himself. She was pretty sure she'd never heard him utter more than two words in a row other than to ask her if she ever stopped talking. All the grizzly vibes in the world told her and every other ranger in Zion he was as cuddly as a porcupine. He wasn't the kind of man to pretend to be someone he wasn't, and that had her wanting to get a closer look. To figure out how he got away with it. He was unforgiving, a little broody. Blunt. Not a guy who would ever look at her twice, let alone take her to that cute coffee shop in town on a date.

In fact, she was fairly certain he hated her guts, based on her few attempts to get to know him and the glares he threw her way anytime she managed get within a couple feet of him.

She wasn't even the sole focus of all that intensity. Zion rangers had all learned to keep their distance, going out of their way to avoid partnering up with Branch as much as possible.

But there were times when she swore she could feel his eyes on her. Watching her every move. It came in goose bumps and shivers throughout the days she worked the trails. But the moment she tried to catch him, he'd be gone. Halfway convincing her she imagined it.

Tanned skin accentuated the rise and valley of muscle in Branch's forearms as he settled the victim's remains in the body bag.

Victim. That was what Sarah Lantos was now. Her

fall hadn't been an accident; she'd been stabbed. Another murder to add to the books while the park was just barely recovering from the last one.

Branch shoved to his full height, around six-four. An entire intimidating foot taller than her frame, and every cell in her body took notice. Her brain had no trouble imagining what it would feel like to have all that muscle pressed against her, how he could easily toss her from one end of her trailer to the other. How he'd take control and—

Crap. He was looking at her with those dark eyes again, as if she'd broadcasted her thoughts.

She let a sugar-sweet smile take its place on her face. Innocent. Unbothered. Airheaded. Lila knew exactly what Branch thought of her—what every ranger in this park thought of her, including Risner—and she let them. Despite her unrequited crush on the man currently scoffing at her, it was far better for all of them to keep their distance than to see through the mask.

Risner clapped his hands together as if he'd done a lick of work helping that poor woman into the body bag. "Jordan, I want you to take Branch up to Scout Lookout and see what you can find by way of evidence. Now that we know our hiker was stabbed, there might be something there we can hand over to law enforcement. Get this taken care of and make sure to clear the trail while you're at it."

Noooooooo. It took everything Lila had not to growl. Or to look at the man who frequently starred in the wayward fantasies she used to get herself to sleep every night. Her skin felt too hot and too tight at the same time as she shifted her weight between her boots. Any time spent alone with Branch Thompson would only end in frustration and an emptiness she hadn't figured out how to get rid of. "I think you meant Sayles. Or…" Lila searched for someone—anyone—she could put in Risner's path, but they'd all taken to crowd control or running while they had the chance. Cowards. "...anyone else."

"Right. Wouldn't want you to chip your manicure." Branch's smirk only served to up her heart rate.

Hot anger pushed to the surface. She didn't give a damn about her manicure. Lila took a step toward him but stopped herself short of pummeling that smirk off his face. She'd built this facade for a reason. She couldn't break, but for some reason she couldn't fathom, he'd somehow gained the ability to pry up her carefully laid scales.

Adding a psychotic twist to her smile, Lila locked her gaze on him. "I've been washing bloodstains off my clothes for years. Yours wouldn't be a burden."

Branch's mouth hitched higher. Almost into a smile. If a grizzly bear summoned from the bowels of hell was capable of smiling.

"Jordan, move. Now. And how many times do I have to tell you to stop altering your uniform? Get rid of the pink, or I'm writing you up a third time. We're federal agents. It's time you start acting like it, or I will find someone who can follow orders." Risner headed after the medical examiner and the body strung between her and another ranger. "For crying out loud. You look like someone threw up a bottle of Pepto Bismol."

Her jaw ached from the pressure of her clenched back teeth. Heat that had nothing to do with the arching sun burned in her neck and cheeks. It was true Risner had a dedicated dislike for her pink accessories, but it'd been months since his last reprimand. And she hated that it had to be in front of Branch. The urge to pull at her kerchief brought her hand to her neck, but she caught herself before giving in. The pink was ridiculous. She knew that, but without it…

Lila turned for the trail that would take her and Branch up the ascent. "We better get moving if we want to make it to the top before sunset."

She didn't bother looking to see if he followed. She could feel him at her back. If she was being honest with herself, she could always feel him. Like her body had somehow attuned to his since her crush had started all those months ago. Traitor.

Though he kept his distance. He always did.

Her usual need to fill the silence failed as she ascended the melty rocks leading onto the permitted portion of the trail. *Third time's the charm.* Now that the medical examiner had concluded Sarah Lantos had been murdered, they'd have to ensure every hiker they encountered left the trail as soon as possible. A killer was on the loose. And it could be anyone, but that was for the law enforcement rangers to deal with. All she had to do was search for evidence Sarah Lantos hadn't gone over that cliff by accident.

"Does he always talk to you like that?" Branch's voice cut through the incessant spiral of thoughts in her head.

It took her a moment to remember this wasn't her every day shift. That she wasn't out here alone and that she had a persona to uphold. Dang. She was losing her touch. Or maybe some of Branch's personality had rubbed off on her today. "Who? Risner? He's the district ranger. I think being an ass is part of his job description."

A growl reached her ears, and she found herself searching the trail for a wild animal. Then realized it came from Branch. Why did she all of a sudden want to feel that growl vibrate through her? Oh, maybe she could add that to her sleep fantasies tonight.

She swallowed the groan working up her throat. Pathetic. This whole crush was just pathetic. Nothing would ever happen between her and Branch Thompson. He'd made that perfectly clear by practically inflating a five-foot-wide bubble between him and everyone around him. The longer she deluded herself that she could break through, the sooner she'd have to check herself into a psychiatric ward. "This next section is a lot steeper than the first half. You're going to want to take your time on the switchbacks. Burning out before you get to the top will only slow us down."

No answer.

Lila subtly—as subtly as she could—craned her chin over one shoulder to ensure she hadn't been talking to herself for the past few minutes. Yep. Branch was still there. Not even looking remotely out of breath or sweaty. *All righty then.*

The switchbacks were the worst, in her opinion. Steep angles, lots of effort, with very little actual elevation gain. Though she didn't hate the hardpacked trail that saw millions of visitors.

Within another thirty minutes, the landscape angled upward as they approached Scout Lookout. Her legs shook under the effort. Three ascents in one day wasn't unheard of for a regular shift, but this one felt different. She didn't want to credit that feeling to the man easily keeping pace with her a few feet back. Instead, she'd pretend it had everything to do with the hiker she'd helped put in a body bag less than a few hours ago. She was good at pretending.

Chains swung ahead of her with a rogue gust of wind. No matter how many times she hiked this trail, there was always a chance she wouldn't make it back down to the Grotto, but a sense of calm settled along her spine.

It had nothing to do with Branch. Nope.

They crested the lookout of Angel's Landing, and Lila set out to ruin the days of three groups of hikers while Branch searched the perimeter of the plateau. No one wanted to spend four hours hiking Zion's most popular trail in one-hundred-degree heat only to be told to go back once you reached the top, but she couldn't take the chance of losing something that might point to Sarah Lantos's killer.

Sarah had set off to climb Angel's Landing at six this morning. She could've been stabbed anytime between ten and now, leaving a whole lot of time for visitors—or the killer—to compromise evidence of the attack.

There was only one place Sarah Lantos could've been stabbed: directly above where her body had been found.

"She was stabbed and thrown over here." Branch stared straight down the cliffside.

"How can you be sure?" Lila stretched her gaze over the side of the cliff, just as she had earlier. Except there was no bright yellow marker telling her a hiker had gone over the edge. There was nothing but the shimmering surface of the Virgin River below and the riverside trail. "The medical examiner moved the body."

He pointed between his feet, a couple inches past the chain lining the lookout. "Because the ground here is stained with blood."

Chapter Four

Something had shifted.

Branch couldn't put his finger on it as he studied Lila across the expanse of dirt that was Scout Lookout. Law enforcement rangers were en route to contain the scene and analyze the blood he'd discovered, but with the sun sinking below the horizon, it would take more than the usual four hours before he and Lila could distance themselves from this trail. Leaving nothing but the two of them and a path of budding stars in the east.

The entire hike to this point had coiled dread so thick in his gut he'd been able to taste the bitterness at the back of his throat. Being alone with Lila Jordan had never worked out in his favor. Her impulsivity, meddling in other peoples' affairs and lack of discipline had left him with more than a few migraines at the end of a shift. Every aspect of her personality sat in opposition to his. It was one of the reasons he'd gone out of his way to ensure their schedules never coincided. He'd managed to switch days and trails with the other park rangers, but Risner had ordered the two of them to search Angel's Landing together. Probably to get Ranger Barbie away from the scene down below.

Except Lila hadn't been her normal upbeat self on the

way up. As if she'd forgotten he was there at all, and all that enthusiasm and pink was nothing but a cover. For the first time, his nervous system hadn't been on the defense around her. He'd been able to relax surrounded by the jaw-dropping views and crystal sky. No personal questions, no attempts to bond, nothing. He'd actually been able to think. About Sarah Lantos, the stab wound, her killer. It'd been...unsettling.

It was no secret Lila had harbored a crush on him these past few months. If he was being honest, most of the female rangers did. He tended to have that effect simply due to the fact he had no real interest in dating or relationships after his divorce. Something about wanting what you couldn't have. He'd gotten used to their personal crusades to help him break out of his shell, to be the one who got him to open up. Unfortunately for them and the rest of the female population, there was nothing inside but a whole lot of self-destructive rage that threatened to blow any minute. Something he only managed to keep locked up by avoiding others. Saving them the fallout.

Lila kicked at a patch of dirt across the Lookout, keeping to herself as they waited for the law enforcement unit. For some awful reason that didn't sit well with him. As if he'd become uniquely tuned to her moods. Which was ridiculous. He should be grateful his ears weren't bleeding from her incessant attempts at humor.

Had the death of a hiker gotten to her? Or had Risner's earlier reprimand thrown off her game?

Dislodging his pack, Branch crouched. They'd ascended and cleared Angel's Landing in five hours and had been waiting for law enforcement for an hour. Not once had he seen her eat anything. Probably some strict diet to control her weight. Wasn't that why most women starved themselves? But she was likely to pass out, and he had no intention of carrying her off this mountain.

"Eat." He tossed one of the protein bars he'd packed in her direction.

Surprisingly, she caught it rather than dodge and squeal as he'd expected. Who was this pod person, and what the hell had she done with Lila? Straightening with the bar in hand, she skimmed her thumbs over the wrapper. "Careful, Branch. Wouldn't want to chip my manicure. I just touched it up this morning."

Ah. There she was. He wasn't sure why he'd bothered. Every ranger in this park was capable of taking care of themselves. They were trained to survive in the wilderness for days on end if necessary and through natural disasters. And yet, by setting aside her zaniness for just a couple minutes, Lila had somehow triggered his instinct to care. A mistake he wouldn't make again. "I'm not carrying you out of here if you pass out."

"Aw." Lila tore into the wrapper, her upper body twisting from one side to the other. A gust of wind whipped her ponytail over one shoulder and consumed his attention as it brushed over her face. "Are you concerned about me, Branch?"

Why did she have to keep repeating his name? His nerves couldn't take it much longer, going from zero to overdrive in the span of a single word out of her mouth. Branch locked his jaw to regain some semblance of control, but that was the thing about Lila. Anytime he found himself around her, that control didn't exist. Like she'd subatomically convinced him to forget years of discipline with her free spirit that left him raw and confused and more than a little angry. He forced himself to focus on cinching his bag and not the way his fingers tingled to brush her hair out of her face.

"I think you secretly like me." She took a bite of the protein bar, chewing with her mouth open while continuing to goad him. "I think all those times you switched shifts with the other rangers to make sure you didn't have to work with me is because you're trying to keep your distance when you really don't want to."

She knew about that? Hell.

Branch shoved to his feet as flashlights flickered down the trail. They were still a ways out, but law enforcement had arrived to take control of the scene. Releasing him from this hell and the demon trying to work her way under his skin. Satan had done an excellent job when he created Lila Jordan. Personalized just for him. "They're here."

"Oh, good. I hope they brought hand warmers." Lila buried the protein bar wrapper in her pack and clapped her hands before heading toward the group of three flashlights. "I'm freezing my butt off."

And what a butt it was. He hadn't been able to avoid getting the perfect view the entire hike up. Say what you will about her eating habits, whatever she was doing had paid off in spades. A tendril of heat spiked through him as he caught another dose. Hell, he was disturbed. In no shape or form should he ever consider Ranger Barbie a good idea. They were coworkers. He'd barely survived his divorce. And she…was everything he didn't want.

Branch settled his pack in place. He hadn't noticed the drop in temperatures, too on edge from maintaining the wall he had to continually reinforce between him and Lila, but the cold seemed to rush him now that she'd escaped his orbit.

"Branch. Jordan." Risner nodded to each of them at

his approach. Two rangers Branch recognized from the scene this afternoon moved past, heading to the Lookout with flashlights and field kits. The law enforcement rangers would take control of the scene, gathering the blood for analysis somewhere off-site, and confirm the samples belonged to their murder victim. "I see you two managed not to kill each other. Not sure how you pulled that off partnering with Jordan here, Branch, but thanks for saving me the paperwork."

He didn't miss the few inches Lila added between her and their district ranger. Or the fleck of hurt in her expression before she smothered it with that smile she pasted on. Which only added to the anger he restrained on a daily basis. And there was that name again. *Jordan.* As if Lila didn't deserve to be humanized by her supervisor. And, well, that just wasn't something he could let continue. "Lila."

He hadn't spoken her name aloud before. The effect was something sweet and light, counter to the bitterness he'd swallowed after taking this assignment.

Risner flicked his flashlight straight into Branch's face. "What was that?"

"Her name is Lila. Not sure why it's so hard for you to remember." The tingling in his fingers was back, except it'd spread to his palms. He curled his hands into fists to keep himself from launching one into Risner's face. "Or do you call the female rangers by their last names as part of whatever sexual harassment settlement you're involved in?"

Even in the last waning rays of sunset, Branch caught the drain of color in Risner's face. "You're out of line, Branch."

"Actually, I prefer to be addressed as woman, demon

or countess." Lila's smile slipped, her gaze bouncing between him and Risner. Pleading with him to drop this. Parted lips he hadn't realized were a bit fuller on one side than the other jumped right back into place. Then again, he hadn't really let himself get too close to notice. For good reason. His blood pressure had crested a few points in the past minute or so. "Whichever comes with the most amount of fear."

The district ranger adjusted his flashlight beam to Lila, rolling his eyes. "Get back down to headquarters, Jordan. You'll find your write-up in your locker, and HR will be waiting for you to discuss the adjustments you've been making to your uniform in the morning."

She motioned toward the two law enforcement rangers. "But the scene—"

"Your shift is over, Ranger." Risner put an end to the conversation. "Your services are no longer required on this case."

"All right." Lila hiked a thumb over her shoulder. "In that case, you might want to tell the law enforcement division about the rope, anchors and carabiners dangling off the north side of the Lookout."

"What?" Risner darted for the edge, pressing up against the chains keeping him from going over. His flashlight locked on something out of Branch's view. "Well, I'll be damned. How did we miss that?"

Branch realized he had made this an uncomfortable situation for Lila. He'd put her in Risner's spotlight without warning her beforehand. Potentially made her position worse. It was clear she was the only one who would suffer the consequences. *Damn it*. She hadn't asked him to fight this battle for her, but he'd made her a target all the same. A growl resonated through his chest as he maneuvered down the rocky incline. This was why he didn't get involved. Why he kept to himself and made it clear he didn't play nice with others. It took more than a few steps for his control to slip back into place.

"Branch, not you, bud. I need you to show us where you found the blood." Risner's voice was nearly lost to the great valleys absorbing the sound of the wild, but there was no way Branch could ignore it.

Lila unpacked her own flashlight and headed down the decline without looking back. Angel's Landing was easily one of the park's most dangerous trails, but she moved with the certainty of a ranger who'd memorized every threat in the terrain. She'd been dismissed, and the heaviness in her shoulders testified to the treatment she and the rest of the female rangers had become accustomed to under Risner's supervision.

This didn't feel right. Lila was the first to realize Sarah Lantos had been stabbed. Not to mention she'd discovered the rope and anchors wedged along the Lookout that could've been utilized by the killer to escape while Branch guarded a meager pool of blood. Ranger Barbie—as much as he hated to admit it—saw more than she let on, and Branch wanted to know why she let her coworkers and supervisor think less.

Of all the rangers in the park, she should be the one to see this through. She'd earned it. He searched the stars for patience. Finding none, he turned back to the district ranger. Branch nodded toward Lila's retreating flashlight. "Assign Lila to the case."

"No way. You have experience with homicides from your time at the Grand Canyon. You're the clear choice here." Risner hiked his hands to his waist with a clear shake of his head. "What the hell has gotten into you,

Branch? I thought I could count on you to keep Jordan in line. Now you're defending her? She's a nobody. You know she doesn't care about this job or take it seriously. Not like we do. You really want Sarah Lantos's family relying on her to get them answers?"

Branch gritted his teeth against the blatant backstabbing and the disrespect of a fellow ranger. Stepping up to Risner, he rode that line between letting the rage surface and walking away. "I'll work your homicide case. Because you're right. Sarah Lantos's family deserves answers, and I've worked homicides in a national park. But I'm not doing it without Lila Jordan."

Chapter Five

Ugh. Feelings.

No amount of Cherry Garcia was going to fix this.

Her body hurt from climbing to Angel's Landing three times in the span of twelve hours of a single day, but worse, she couldn't get back to that lovely space where she didn't have to feel anything. The one place she felt safe. Numb.

The house creaked from another gust. The twelve-hundred-square-foot ranch-style house she and Sayles shared in the Watchman government housing development—when her roommate bothered to sleep here at all—was little more than a cardboard box with two bedrooms and a single bathroom. Updates hadn't been done in years, roaches and mouse droppings weren't uncommon, and a good portion of her sleep terrors occurred right in this very room. But it was only a quarter mile from headquarters.

Despite how often she and Sayles cleaned, there was no getting the stains out of the combination tub/shower or rid of the permanent smell of mildew. But they had put in a lot of effort to personalize everything without painting—that was against the rental agreement.

Risner's Pepto Bismol remark might not fully apply

to the flares of pink in her uniform, but it certainly applied to her bedroom. Her twin-size comforter looked as though it'd been skinned straight off a pink Muppet with matching pillows and poofs. Lampshade, check. Curtains, check. Most of her casual outfits? Check. In the famous words of Julia Roberts in *Steel Magnolias*, pink was her signature color.

It was the only thing that kept her heart from turning all the way black.

Risner. She scowled merely thinking of his name. Lila scooped another double spoonful of Cherry Garcia and shoved it into her mouth, relaxing on the secondhand couch she and Sayles had found on the side of the road in Springdale. This place wasn't anything extravagant, but it was theirs. Hers. Someplace no one could find her.

There were those feelings again. The ones she'd managed to ignore since coming to Zion, but the little buggers just didn't get the message she wasn't interested. Chocolate chunks and cherries weren't going to touch this. She needed something stronger.

The romantic comedy she'd chosen for tonight—and almost every night—helped. The lonely, isolated, nerdy main character was getting all dolled up and waxed clean to enter a beauty pageant in order to catch a bomber. She just happened to find love along the way in another FBI agent, and right there was that shrapnel of hope Lila couldn't afford. That her self-isolation and loneliness would end in happily-ever-after.

Images blurred on the screen as her mind drifted back to Branch Thompson for the hundredth time tonight. He'd corrected Risner's use of her last name, though she wasn't sure why. In what world did Branch do anything that didn't involve scowling, growling or prowling? It didn't make sense and had ultimately landed her higher on Risner's hit list. The district ranger had removed her from the investigation in retaliation.

It was just as well. What did she know about murder? Her expertise—as far as her supervisor and coworkers were aware—extended to pairing the right eyeshadow to her uniform, coating herself in sunscreen because *ew, wrinkles* and changing out her boot laces with a pop of color.

No one took her seriously. And that was the way she liked it.

Pounding registered on the front door.

Her entire nervous system flinched at the onslaught, and she nearly dropped her Cherry Garcia on her favorite blanket. Dribbles of ice cream slid down her chin. She wiped it with the back of her sweatshirt sleeve. "Who is it?"

"Branch." His voice was throaty and low.

Nope. Not what she was expecting. Her heart rate shot into overdrive. She scrambled to clean up her face, smooth down her hair and make it look as though she hadn't spent the last three hours trying to drown her sorrows in calories. Then again, maybe he'd feel better she'd eaten, considering he'd gifted her that protein bar earlier.

His presence practically bled through the thin wood door. "You still there?"

She didn't know. Maybe this was an out-of-body experience. Or a dream. Never in all his time at Zion had Branch crossed the development from his house to hers.

"Um, just a second!" Squealing. Sure. That was the way to go. Lila nearly tripped over her extra thick fuzzy socks as she rushed to the front door. She scanned the house with her hand on the doorknob. There was no saving the Netflix-and-chill vibe she'd lost herself in, but at least it didn't smell like animal carcass in here. She wrenched the door inward, setting sights on the mountain of a man she had to remind herself would only visit for official reasons. "Uh, hi. Who died? I mean, who else died? I mean, what can I do for you in the middle of the night, Branch?"

What wouldn't she do was more like it.

He answered with a low growl that could mean anything from *I don't understand your joke* to *I only speak to animals* as he stepped past her into the house.

She gestured over the threshold behind his back. "Won't you come inside?"

He didn't fit here. Though she imagined he didn't really fit anywhere given his size. It worked well for him out in the open, but in her tiny-ass house that she had to share with a roommate to afford? Not so much.

Branch surveyed her kingdom as she closed the door behind him. She'd changed out of her uniform into one of her oversize T-shirts from a secondhand shop in Springdale. Sans pants. This was going really well for her tonight. He watched a few seconds of the movie before taking in the melting ice cream and discarded spoon on the scuffed wood coffee table.

Then took a seat on her couch she was sure struggled to support his weight and grabbed what was left of her Cherry Garcia and the single spoon. That she'd eaten off of. "I love this movie."

"What is happening?" Lila slapped both cheeks, trying to wake herself up. Because there was no way in hell Branch Thompson—Mr. Don't Look at Me if You Don't Want a Tree Shoved Down Your Throat—was sitting on her couch, eating her ice cream and watching her favorite movie. She must've died on Angel's Landing today. Yeah. That made more sense. She was dead, and this was her purgatory.

"Sit down." Branch nodded toward the butt imprint on her side of the couch.

Lila didn't know what else to do. Rounding the coffee table, legs bare and a little prickly, she lowered herself onto the couch beside him, careful to keep a minimum of six inches between them. She sat stiff as a board, her mouth dry. She tried to clear her throat, but two pints of Ben & Jerry's had the unexpected ability to make that impossible.

"As much as I loved our time together today, Branch, my shift is over. I'm a free woman for the next six hours, and I'm curious as to why you're here. In my house. Eating my ice cream."

"Did you want more?" He offered her the container, only to reveal less than a bite left. Rude. Settling back into the thin couch cushions, Branch spread his legs in front of him as though he had nowhere else to be. Or like he made it a habit to visit her in the middle of the night.

"I'm good." No. Her voice did not just crack on that last word. Closing her eyes against the rush of heat in her face and neck, Lila tried to get a handle on herself. Then she set her full attention on him.

Shadows had settled under his eyes, deepening the lines in the corners. Like he was in the kind of pain no one could fix. His shoulders seemed tighter, and it took everything in her not to offer to rub out the tension. He wouldn't appreciate being touched, and honestly, no matter how many times she'd fantasized about this exact moment—having him in her house—this entire situation made her nervous as hell. Maybe she hadn't actually accomplished scrubbing the day off in her too-hot shower until her skin turned raw.

"Are you a serial killer?" She'd never seen an attractive serial killer, but if they were out there, she bet they would look just like him.

Branch turned those dark eyes on her. His mouth twitched at one side as if she'd surprised him. Then again, maybe he got accused of committing murder all time. She didn't know. She didn't know anything about him. The man wasn't exactly keen on engaging with society. "No."

"Okay." She dragged the word out longer than necessary to try to get her brain in drive. "So if you're not here to kill me, what are you doing in my house?"

Setting the now empty pint on the coffee table with a last lick of the spoon, he scanned her house. Though she couldn't imagine what it was he was looking for. All these government houses had the same floor plan and upgrades, which meant he was looking at an identical layout as his. "You're back on the case."

That…was not what she expected to come out of his mouth. Shock held her brain hostage for a minute. Maybe two.

Branch didn't seem to mind the resulting silence.

Then she couldn't stop the torrent as though she'd finally been released from a year-long vow of silence. "I don't… I don't understand. Risner sent me back to headquarters. He wrote me up and told me to make sure I met with HR in the morning. As of three hours ago, I was convinced I was being fired. What could have changed?"

For the first time, Branch met her gaze without so much as a wince at the sound of her voice. And waited for her to connect the dots.

"You convinced him to keep me." She braced herself

for the argument, but it never came. The gritty, peeling fabric of her couch rubbed against the backs of her thighs as a whole new level of awareness coursed through her. She didn't know what to think about that, what to do. He'd gone against their district ranger to call Risner out for his blatant sexism she and the rest of the female rangers had to put up with for this job. Now this? "Why would you do that? You can't stand me."

Branch shoved to stand up, pushing the couch back a few inches at the effort. He stared down at her. Not intimidating. Just…there. Like he would sign up to fight all of her battles if he could, even the ones she'd kept to herself. Which didn't make a lick of sense. He didn't answer for a series of moments. She wasn't sure if he would at all. Until all that intensity centered on her. "Why do you let everyone think you're something you're not?"

"Because the truth is too awful." A rush of shame burned hot under her skin. It took longer than she wanted for her to make sense of what he was saying—what he thought he knew about her—and for a split second, she was tired of lying. Of being exactly what people expected of her. If anyone was going to see through the lies she'd sprinkled like breadcrumbs over the years, she'd put her hope on Branch Thompson. Only to have been disappointed over and over again when he ignored and flat out rejected her.

He hadn't fought Risner for her to remain on the case out of some mutual interest or a potential friendship as she'd wanted since the day he set foot in Zion. Branch had done it to figure out what happened to Sarah Lantos. Which was kind of admirable in and of itself. Lila fisted her sleep shirt to get her head out of the clouds.

"The Grotto at six." He didn't wait for her to answer as he suddenly lunged for the door. "Don't be late."

Lila couldn't help but scramble after him. "Why? What's at six?"

Branch pulled up short of crossing the threshold back out into the gusty darkness and locked his gaze on her. "We start tracking the killer."

Chapter Six

Lila Jordan was going to be the death of him.

She was late. But had he expected anything less? It seemed in the years she'd joined the National Park Service, she'd gone out of her way to rebel against any and all authority, protocol and human decency. As far as Branch could tell, her erratic monologues and meddling were about holding onto some kind of individuality while conforming to a group for a paycheck. He imagined she was the child who never followed the rules, managed to bring nothing but chaos within her family and played pranks on her siblings and parents.

But with a smile like the one that haunted his dreams, she probably swayed anyone and everyone into her line of thinking with the promise of a good time and a little spice thrown in.

Hell, even some of their fellow rangers looked at her as though some of her stardust could rub off on them, but no one compared to the enigma that was Ranger Barbie. There were just some things that couldn't be learned. Lila's daring was one of them. In the end, that daring and outright disobedience would only serve to distance her from any real connections. Because how could you trust someone who didn't follow a typical pattern of behavior and made decisions based on their emotions?

But hadn't he transferred to Zion National Park to find that same distance? Maybe Lila had a point.

The cold seeped through his uniform as he stared out over the Virgin River. The current this far into the canyon wasn't as strong as it would be upstream, but it reached depths of well over fifteen feet in some places, and hikers never seemed to have the good sense to follow direction on calm days like this. The sun was already rising in the east but had yet to reach the canyon floor. Everything about the view settled that invisible burn of rage he had to keep at bay for the sake of his sanity. This place—the isolation, the beauty, the work—it all combined to fight against his natural instincts to bring down the world around him. After all, it was only fair after what the world had done to him.

Two taps registered on his shoulder, and Branch spun to face the threat.

"Morning! Sorry I'm a few minutes late, but I thought we could warm up with coffee. It's really more for your safety. I'm not a people person until I hit the bottom of the first cup of caffeine."

Ah. The mask was back in place. This wasn't the Lila he'd met on the trail to Scout Lookout yesterday. Ranger Barbie had returned. In full force it seemed.

Handing off one of the cups she held, she took a sip from her own. She'd tied her hair back beneath her Stetson again, accentuating a sharp, feminine jawline. Thick lashes dusted the tops of her cheekbones, and those almond-shaped blue eyes felt as though could see straight through him. There was no denying the natural beauty he'd noted last night. In fact, seeing her in that sleep shirt with an ice cream stain below her chin had probably been one of the most gut-wrenching experiences of his life. Because for those short minutes, Lila had just been herself. Effortless and open, if not a little paranoid when it came to serial killers. "I had to guess on the way you take it. I figured black. Like your soul."

She wasn't wrong. Branch took the offering. The bitterness of the coffee failed to cut through the sweetness rolling off her in waves. Actually, he wasn't sure if there was anything that could protect him against the onslaught of Ranger Barbie's full powers. He could almost see the sound wall of bubble-gum pink and high-pitched laughter coming straight at him. "Thanks."

That bright smile that felt a little too forced at times transformed her face from morning zombie to cocaine high. Damn, the whiplash between her two personalities triggered a painful knot in his neck. Again, that tendril of curiosity tightened in his chest. It had started yesterday on their hike up Angel's Landing, convincing him he'd witnessed something he wasn't supposed to. The real her.

So what made a woman like Lila go out of her way to lie to bosses and coworkers? Surely it didn't extend to the people in her personal life, so why here at the park?

She hiked her shoulders higher, studying the Grotto with its fifty-foot trees, asphalted paths and worn, wooden picnic tables.

The park itself remained open twenty-four-seven, but the shuttle system to get visitors this far into the park had only just begun for the day. It would be another fifteen minutes or so before this trail was overrun. While Sarah Lantos's death had been determined to be homicide, law enforcement rangers didn't have the pull to shut down the Angel's Landing trail. Their only saving grace would be the lottery system that limited the amount of hikers.

Lila seemed to sense their limited opportunity to get moving without an audience. "So what's the plan, Stan? I've got three days' worth of supplies and sixteen ounces of caffeine in me. If we don't start hiking, I might have to climb the side of the Lookout to burn it all off."

She'd come prepared. Good. Neither of them could risk going into this unprepared, but based on his previous homicide experience, he didn't expect that the killer had remained in the park, either.

"Whoever stabbed Sarah Lantos either climbed the Lookout to get to his victim or used the rope and anchors up the side as an escape after he killed her." Branch was already moving across the road as the first shuttle curved along the main transit vein of the park toward the start of the Angel's Landing trail.

"Don't forget he also pushed her over the edge." Her tone was a bit too enthusiastic for this conversation and time of day. "I'm betting the former. The anchors and carabiners would've already had to have been in place for him to escape without any other hikers seeing him flee, which means he most likely climbed the Lookout and set his route in the days leading up to her murder. He would've had to make camp at the base or use a sleep platform."

She was right. Damn it. Why hadn't he thought of that? "You climb?"

"You don't?" The barb hit as she no doubt intended. There were a limited number of climbing rangers throughout the National Park Service. She obviously enjoyed knowing this was one area she outranked him. Lila twisted her pack to her front and unzipped the top, showcasing a perfectly coiled rope of blue fiber with yellow and green woven in. "It's been years since I've free climbed. We could use the killer's gear, but I brought my own in case we don't want to trust another climber's routine."

"If he escaped down Scout Lookout, why bother inspecting his gear and anchor points?" Branch picked up the pace as he hauled himself up the thin rocks layered one on top of the other. Like melted chocolate. His muscles still protested against yesterday's ascent while Lila looked as though she could run a marathon straight up the damn mountain. In reality, there was no best way to get straight to the base of Angel's Landing from here. They'd have to climb either way.

"A climber's routine can tell you a lot about a person. Fitness level, climbing experience, discipline, how often they need to rest. A good majority of free climbers make national parks their Everest. They want to tick as many as possible off the list, sometimes even forgoing the legal route in order to conquer a mountain. Like Yosemite. It's illegal to climb certain parks, in which case there might be an arrest record. We can take all that information and compare it to past permits at the other parks, too, to get an ID on our suspect." She attacked the rise in elevation without so much as a change in her breathing, as if Mattel's CEO was personally waiting for her at the top with a new Barbie. "I imagine Sarah Lantos's killer didn't bother filing for a permit to make the hike, so we'll have to use other ways to locate a suspect. Don't you think?"

Okay. He hadn't thought of that, either. He'd worked a homicide as a law enforcement ranger in Grand Canyon for years before landing in Zion, but the rest frequency and climbing experiences of solo climbers were beyond his scope. "You were a climbing ranger."

Though not here in Zion. She had to have worked for

one of the other parks. Joshua Tree. Arches. Maybe Red Rock. Except then why would Risner keep her as an entry-level ranger if she had that kind of experience?

"No. Climbing for me was a form of therapy. You know, the kind of therapy that shuts off your brain because you have to focus on not dying, and you don't have to give up your secrets to a stranger. Way better than that psychotherapy crap, in my opinion."

"Can't say I don't disagree." Despite his insistence on attending marriage counseling and family therapy in the months leading up to the end of his marriage, Branch had realized too late he and his ex-wife had passed the stage of help. There'd been nothing left to save. "What else do you use as therapy?"

What the hell did he care? It wasn't like they were partners. They were barely more than acquaintances. Professionals. Nothing more. And yet, he'd somehow deemed it necessary to surprise her at her house in the middle of the night to inform her of her ongoing involvement in this case.

"Lots of things." She easily kept pace ahead of him by a few feet. "Yoga, playing violin, ice-skating lessons. Oh, I ran a marathon a couple years ago, but I wouldn't do it again."

"And now?" Branch wanted to punch himself in the face. He'd spent the past four months keeping his distance and setting the parameters of their working relationship. But since witnessing her slip yesterday on this very trail, the harder he tried to gain back that coldness, the faster it trickled through his fingers. The need to figure out the puzzle she presented called to him on a primal level, and it seemed there was nothing he could do about it until he got his answer. That was all this was: a puzzle he wanted to solve.

They were moving into the switchbacks, making great time, but there was still a matter of four hours between their position and the end of the trail.

"Now I'm kind of lost." Her voice had dropped, away from the pitch only canines could hear. It'd only been hours since he'd left her in that run-down house the government deemed safe, and he was already craving another glimpse of the woman Ranger Barbie tried to suffocate. "And I'm tired."

Living two separate lives birthed an exhaustion that had the tendency to sink bone-deep and refuse to let up until enough time without pressure passed. He'd felt it while pretending his marriage still had a chance. Showing the world one person—a man happily married and in love with his wife—as reality sucked the life from him.

He wasn't sure how long Lila had been trying to hold it together, but it'd only taken a few months before he succumbed to the crushing fatigue. Life sure as hell hadn't asked his permission before it decided to blow up in his face, and now he was stuck.

Just like Lila.

Chapter Seven

The killer had known exactly what he was doing. He was experienced and knew his route up the side of Scout Lookout better than the rangers who practically lived in this park. The bolts he'd drilled into the cliffside for his anchors were doing a masterful job of remaining in place despite Branch's dangling weight.

Their killer was experienced, but he would've been better off taking his rope with him during his escape to avoid potential DNA testing. So why hadn't he? Had he needed a quick getaway and couldn't afford the extra weight? Or had he left it on purpose?

Lila touched down at the base of Angel's Landing first, her harness digging between her thighs and around her hips. Hands dusted with chalk, she brushed the excess on her uniform slacks. That was really going to piss Risner off.

Having her descend the killer's route had been the most efficient use of their draining energy after four hours of hiking vertically. Using the killer's anchors and carabiners, she'd secured her own rope to the cliff face as Branch lowered her at an excruciatingly slow pace as though afraid he might drop her at any moment. Which had been a possibility, but a part of her trusted him more than she trusted herself.

She couldn't make out his features from six thousand feet below, but she could imagine him using his best grizzly bear impression to scare people off. Unholstering the radio at her hip, she pressed the push-to-talk button with little hope her signal would escape the surrounding mountains. "Ranger Jordan to Ranger Thompson. Your turn. Over."

Static crackled through the speaker. One second. Two. The high whistle of the wind cutting through all these surrounding peaks and valleys cut through her concentration as she stared up at his outline.

"I'm good." A man of few words and even less humor. She couldn't get enough.

Lila allowed herself to relive the gravel in his voice. Was that nerves? Damn, he was killing her down here. She studied him while opening the channel. "I promise not to drop you. If I wanted you dead, I would've used the candles I lit last night as part of a sacrificial ritual in your honor."

"You're not funny." Another crackle from the radio. Or was that a crack in his voice?

Widening her legs to take more of his weight—because she was going to get him off this mountain come hell or high water—she locked the end of the rope near her dominant hip. She couldn't stop the laugh bursting from her chest. She'd never thought there would be a day when the great Branch Thompson showed vulnerability. She was pretty sure the man did anything he could to avoid it, and he sure as hell wouldn't want that vulnerability made public. "I'm pretty funny."

No answer to that.

She kept her squinting gaze on him, noting the position of the sun. Shade bathed her in cooler temperatures, but time hadn't been on their side since Sarah Lantos's murder. "How do you plan to get down here if you don't trust me to take your weight? Maybe you shouldn't have eaten my Ben & Jerry's last night."

Okay. Now she was just poking the bear, but she couldn't resist getting under that guarded man's skin. Just felt right in the moment.

"You shouldn't shame people for their food choices." The rope tugged in her hand.

"All right. How about this." Why did she suddenly feel like a hostage negotiator? Maybe that should be her next area of study. Something new to keep her mind busy while she tried to figure out how to get this black abyss out of the middle of her chest. "I will buy you your own pint of Cherry Garcia that you can eat in the dark with no one else around. I'll even lend you my DVD of the movie we watched last night."

"You're the only person I know who still uses DVDs." He was stalling, and they both knew it.

But she was going to let that comment slide. It was the least she could do considering she'd discovered a new species of grizzly bear that could speak more than two words at a time. "I've checked all the bolts and anchors. They are perfectly capable of handling your weight."

His outline shifted overhead. They were killing daylight here. Every second he refused to trust her was another second Sarah Lantos's killer remained free. Was it really so much to ask to trust the woman you'd despised for the better part of four months? "Now you're shaming my weight."

She couldn't win. Lila raised the radio to her mouth

to counter. But stopped short. The hairs on the back of her neck stood on end, her scalp tightening in warning. As though she was being watched. Shifting her weight to dislodge the sensation, she searched for the source. There wasn't a whole lot to study, but there were countless ridges, shadows and shrubbery to hide in. A shiver chased down her spine. They'd set out to track a killer, but what if the killer was tracking them? "Get down here."

The change in her voice must have been apparent. Without a response, the slack slid from the rope, tightening with Branch's weight. Exposed to the rope's fiber, the friction against the raw skin of her hands threatened to leave her with burns, but she wouldn't compromise Branch's descent because of a little pain. She'd demanded he trust her. This was him trusting her.

His full weight tugged at the harness strapped at her hips, bringing her to her toes. One wrong move, and she could face-plant against the side of the cliff as he free-fell, though she was fairly certain she wouldn't drop him. Seventy-five—no, eighty percent sure. This was why it was a good idea to climb with a partner around your same size, which begged the question: Of all the rangers at his disposal, why had Branch fought for her to be part of this hunt?

Lila kept her gaze upward. Minutes stretched into hours of repetition: the rope sliding through her gloved hands, the mental check-ins on his progress, the lactic burn in her arms. Sweat built at her temples, but he'd only reached the halfway point. Pressure expanded in her chest and hadn't let up. It was growing stronger. As if whoever was watching had somehow gotten closer without her realizing. Her breath shallowed as she tried to split her attention between Branch and the presence at her back. She couldn't risk a single mistake with his life in her hands.

Her arms shook with the effort to keep Branch from falling to his death, but they were making progress. He was almost on the ground, and the closer he got, the less the pressure in her chest had power over her. The fact that his harness accentuated the muscles running the length of his thighs and rear with every movement didn't hurt, either.

When he touched down, the rope slackened between them—taking both a physical and a mental weight off her body—and she rushed to meet him, throwing her arms around his neck. "Look at that. You did it!"

A wave of tension tightened every muscle under her touch, from his shoulders to his toes. The air charged with something she couldn't name, but it was far from the friendly conversation they'd engaged in during the descent down the cliff face.

Branch shoved out of her hold, expression shut down. Eyes hooded. His chest rose violently. "Don't touch me."

The inky blackness she tried to keep under wraps below layers and layers of pink and bubbles threatened to escape. Air lodged in her throat at the sudden change in his demeanor, and the banter between them a little while ago vanished as though it never happened in the first place. Had she imagined it? She had the tendency to do that. To see connections and relationships as more than they really were. "I'm sorry. I didn't mean—"

"It doesn't matter what you meant." Branch loosened his harness, stepping out of it and leaving it behind. No, shoving it away as though it would come to life and bite him. He maneuvered around her without so much as a second glance at her. Why did that hurt more than his words? "We need to keep moving."

Lila stared after him, not really knowing what to do as he searched the ground around them. She'd made a mistake. Believed he'd started letting down his standoffish guard. For her.

She stopped herself from clenching her hands. They ached from acting as base to his descent. What did she think was going to happen when she hugged him? That he'd suddenly see she'd been right there in front of him this whole time? Forget he hadn't ignored and pushed her away since he came to Zion? A nauseous churn erupted in her stomach. All too familiar and suffocating. Rejection. Shame. Worthlessness.

Shucking her own harness, she folded and packed it in her pack, unwilling to leave it behind as Branch had done with his. The killer. They were tracking a killer. Analyzing what had changed between them from last night to a few minutes ago wouldn't get them any closer to finding Sarah Lantos's killer. It would be okay. She'd survived the mess she'd made of her family. She would survive Branch's indifference.

Her boot caught on a rock, and she pitched forward. The world ripped out from beneath her.

Lila threw her palms out to catch herself, but a massive wall of muscle stepped between her and the ground. Strong hands secured her hips and steadied her on her feet.

Her breath escaped her chest for an entirely different reason than Branch running as though she'd physically disgusted him. But it was the heat singeing her insides beneath his palms that threw her off-balance.

Drawing herself to her full height—at least a head shorter than Branch, his chest pressed to hers—she locked her gaze on his. The hardness had left his expression, leaving the man who'd set himself in front of her TV with her favorite ice cream last night.

She set her hand against his chest to return to the distance he'd set between them. "Thanks."

"It's not personal." Calloused fingers tightened on her hips, keeping her in place. His body heat seared through the thin cotton of her uniform's button-down. It was made worse by the increasing temperatures as the sun arced higher in the sky. "I haven't let anyone touch me since my divorce."

"I didn't know." Divorce—no matter the circumstances—was hard. It changed people. While she hadn't been through it, she'd witnessed friends' entire lives crumple when a marriage ended. Couples she'd admired for their commitment and those stolen glances at each other when they thought no one was looking had suddenly turned bitter and angry and hostile, until they were no longer recognizable. And Branch was one of its victims.

Lila counted off his heartbeats against her palm, steady and strong. Just like him. "But it's a little hard to believe you don't like to be touched when you're still holding onto me."

Distinct lines deepened between his brows as if he couldn't possibly figure out why he hadn't let go. In Lila's next breath, Branch seemed to come back to himself and retreated a step, but the impression of his hands refused to dissolve. "I'm sorry. I'm not... I'm not good at being around people anymore."

"Everyone has cuddle-with-a-toaster-in-the-bathtub days." Brushing invisible wrinkles from her uniform, she set her performance smile in place, trying to lighten the mood. She'd been doing it for so long, it'd become as easy as breathing. Because it was better than letting the darkness win again. She didn't expect him to tell her about his divorce, and she wouldn't push. But the idea of someone hurting this man set her teeth.

Lila readjusted her pack on her shoulders. Unnecessarily, of course, but she'd achieved satisfactory distraction level. There weren't any signs of a campsite around here. The killer must've moved deeper into the valley.

"Don't." That single word rocked through her as Branch ate up the distance he'd put between them. She felt the roughness in his voice deep in her bones.

Time slowed as he raised his knuckles to brush against one corner of her mouth. "Don't put that fake smile on, Lila. You don't ever have to hide from me."

Chapter Eight

What was happening to him? An internal battle raged, pulling him in two directions. One side retreated into the safety of his no-personal-attachments rule, and the other closed the distance between him and Lila.

He'd told her he didn't like to be touched, and yet he couldn't seem to stop himself from reaching out. From trying to rid the world of that protective layer she pasted in place, hiding herself from him and everyone else. What the hell did it matter to him how she lived her life? And why couldn't he get rid of that part of him that wanted to know what had conditioned her to don that pink armor? What didn't she want him to see?

Branch dropped his hand away from Lila's mouth as panic flared in those sky blue eyes.

She slid out of his reach, her disguise back in full force. It was terrifying and impressive at the same time, how easily she could switch from one personality to the other. She hiked her pack higher on her shoulders. That bright pink manicure stood out against the drabness of her uniform.

The gray and dark green washed her out. If anything, the small pops of pink only added to her beauty. How hadn't he noticed that before? Oh, right. Because he was making it his personal mission to never speak to another human being again.

"I'm not seeing signs of a campsite here. We should keep moving. Pick up the killer's tracks before he gets too far into backcountry." Lila raised her hands to her hips.

She was going to pretend he hadn't broken his own rule by touching her. All right. He could pretend, too. Branch growled his approval.

"Oh, good. You're growling at me." She moved ahead of him, pack in place, the rope and gear she'd supplied professionally stowed.

His mouth twitched before he could stop it. Her sarcasm and teasing just hit right. He couldn't explain it.

And he couldn't explain how the nerves that held him hostage on his descent down Angel's Landing had lost their intensity now that he had his feet on the ground. His fingers still ached from the pressure he'd kept on the radio. He'd been hanging on for dear life—physically and mentally—but Lila's encouragement had done something to him. Something he hadn't expected. It was as though his entire body had tuned to the sound of her voice, and all he'd been able to think about was rappelling as fast as possible to get another dose of her brightness and humor. Her half-hearted death threats and ability to distract him from the darkness in his head.

Without her, he wasn't sure he would've made it down at all, and wasn't that ironic considering he'd done everything in his power to avoid Ranger Barbie over the past four months? Deep down, he knew why the distance had been necessary. He'd known how dangerous Lila Jordan was before she'd even introduced herself and offered to buy him coffee as a welcome-to-the-team gesture. He'd felt that danger at the top of the cliff and again as he'd allowed himself that brief physical connection a couple minutes ago, a craving to be near her, to give up this damn fight he'd taken on after his divorce. While he had no intention of ever being vulnerable in a relationship again, Lila didn't deserve his rough side.

"She cheated on me." He wasn't sure he'd ever spoken the words out loud before, but he noted the hitch in Lila's step ahead of him. To her credit, she covered herself well, pushing forward as though he wasn't spilling his guts. "My ex-wife and my best friend. Guess it'd been happening for a few months. Right under my nose. At the time, I thought we were happy. Nothing seemed off until I caught them together."

"I'm sorry." Lila's elbows tucked closer to her rib cage. She kept her head down to the point he couldn't read her. Though, if he was being honest, she wasn't like the other rangers who wore their emotions on their sleeves. Even Risner gave away his moods before he opened his mouth. But not Lila. She was an impenetrable force of nature. "Some people's birthstone is crystal meth, and it shows."

"You're not wrong." Damn this woman. It wasn't enough she felt she had to empathize with him, but she had to go and try to make him laugh. Why did she insist on clawing under his skin when he wanted nothing but to disappear? To stay in the dark rather than chase those flashes of spark she set off inside him. "Worse part was, I found out later she was pregnant at the time I walked in on them. With my baby."

"You have a kid?" Her shoulders tensed as though she intended to turn around to face him, but Lila kept hold of herself. Better than he was doing, that was damn sure.

"No." That single word was all he would say about it.

Shade cast over them as they kept to the base of the

mountain, but it was that permanent inner chill that refused to let up. It was windier here in the valley, setting the surrounding weeds and trees in motion, erasing evidence from the dirt with a simple gust. It'd take a miracle for them to pick anything up from their killer.

Branch forced one foot in front of the other, fighting that cavern of hollowness in his chest. "She chose not to keep it. Said she didn't want anything to tie herself to me after the divorce."

And there'd been nothing he could do. Nothing he'd said had swayed his ex to change her mind. She hadn't given him a chance. While they hadn't talked about starting their family yet due to their separate careers, to have the potential taken from him without warning had sent him spiraling.

"Why are you telling me this?" Lila's voice softened, telling him this was the woman he'd glimpsed on the trail yesterday afternoon. The one who'd realized their victim had been murdered, who'd identified the killer's escape and who'd surprised him with the ins and outs of climbing down the cliff face. The real Lila.

In that moment, Branch wanted to see her face. To memorize every centimeter and commit it to memory in case he never got the chance again. This was a rare occurrence that deserved to be remembered, like a comet that only orbited the solar system every few hundred years. "Because I didn't like the look in your eyes when I snapped at you. Like I'd hurt you. I don't want you to think… You don't deserve my anger."

Lila slowed her tread through the scrub brush. Her shoulders rose on a strong inhale as she swiped at her face. "As much as I appreciate that, you don't have to explain yourself to me. We're not friends. We work together. It's not your job to manage my feelings."

Oh hell. Was she crying? His heart threatened to beat straight out of his chest. "Lila, look at me."

Tears glittered in her eyes as she turned to face him.

"Why are you crying?" Something violent tore through his chest at the sight, and he wanted nothing more than to kick his own ass for putting those tears in her eyes. One step. That was all it would take to ease that animal inside of him demanding he fix this. He fought the urge to capture a rogue tear trekking down her face. There was a reason he hadn't opened up to anyone since his divorce. Because of this, right here. Having his pain reflected back at him was akin to falling to his death, slow and unbearable.

"Because I'm mad you had to go through all that, and it's illegal to kill people, and that shit is frustrating." Lila whipped her hands down from her face, rolling her gaze to the sky to dry the last of her tears.

Okay. That was cute. Her frustration on his behalf seeped into him, a wave crashing against the shore and nearly knocking him under the current.

Ranger Barbie wasn't all plastic as he'd been led to believe. She had feelings, and right now, she'd chosen to take on a pain that didn't even belong to her so he didn't have to feel it alone.

Branch took that step, putting himself in her personal space. Hints of her shampoo slapped him in the face on a gust of wind ripping through the canyon. Light and invigorating, it challenged his senses when most everything had gone numb since his divorce. Just like her. The effect awoke sensations he hadn't allowed himself to feel in a long time. Not only had this pink nightmare barged into his life uninvited, she'd somehow convinced him she was essential to coming back to the land of the living. "It's not your job to manage my feelings, either, but I appreciate the effort."

Her brows, a few shades darker than her bleached hair, drew together as though the idea of taking her own advice had never been spelled out for her. The tears dried, and all that was left was a pool of confusion in those sky blue eyes. "You really know how to give off mixed signals."

Branch came back to himself. Remembered why they were out here, in the middle of nowhere, and who they were tracking. And that he couldn't—wouldn't—put himself in a position to get carved up again. He'd barely survived the first time. He wasn't so sure he'd be able to pull himself back together after a second.

And Lila Jordan was capable of ending worlds with a smile on her face and that laugh that followed him into his dreams. Even if it was all a lie. "Turns out I'm not the only one."

Her mouth parted at the jab. It'd been a cheap shot but necessary to keep the professional distance between them. She'd been right before. They weren't friends. They were coworkers. Nothing more. So why did watching her slide into her Barbie persona piss him off so much?

"With all due respect, Ranger Thompson, intercourse yourself." Lila didn't wait for his response, turning back to the path without seeing the grin splitting his face. Was that her professional way of telling him to—

She pulled up short.

Branch's defenses caught the change in her body language, and he maneuvered around her to get a better look ahead.

A campsite.

Abandoned but clear evidence that someone had been there in the past few hours, possibly as early as an hour ago considering the dying embers of the fire. It wasn't anything much—a few rocks set in a circle with blackened twigs and a dead log in the center. What looked like an empty sandwich bag had caught in a bush nearby. Flattened dirt suggested the killer might've rolled out a sleeping bag or mat. Simple. Purely for survival.

Zion didn't accept backcountry permits for this area, nor did it approve of campfires in any capacity. Which meant they were most likely looking at the remnants of the killer's campsite. Streaks cut through the dirt as though the killer had tried to cover his tracks, and from what Branch could make out, there were no identifying treads in the footprints. Like their suspect had filled his boot treads with something to erase anything that could lead to him. "Stay back."

"I would rather take a trailer hitch to the shins." Lila broke through the barrier he'd made between her and the campsite, throwing him off-balance enough to pitch him to one side. Great. Ranger Barbie had gone feral. This was going to end poorly. For him. "I'm trained in search and rescue. Isn't that why you brought me along on this little field trip?"

Right. Not because he'd been intrigued by the pretty demon. Branch scanned the surrounding landscape, unable to pick up any other signs of life. Defeat coated the back of his throat in acid. "It's too late. The killer has already disappeared."

Chapter Nine

There wasn't much left of the campsite. At least nothing that they could use to identify Sarah Lantos's killer. Why had she and Branch been given that responsibility again? They couldn't be the only ones brought into the search. Zion National Park stretched over two hundred and thirty-two square miles. It would take weeks, if not months, to cover that much ground, and even if they got lucky and found a clue as to where the killer had gone, they were at risk out here in the open. Exposure, rock falls, flash floods... So many ways a national park could kill a person. Which meant they were most likely one of several teams involved in the search.

Lila scanned the campsite for something—anything—to give them a direction. This valley branched into several other canyons, each leading in a different direction. While she had her theories as to where a sane person might go from here, it relied solely on whether the killer had done his research of the area, had come prepared or wasn't completely out of his damn mind.

Could anyone who'd taken a person's life be considered in a healthy mental state? She couldn't answer that.

The boot treads left behind weren't anything she'd come across before. Patternless. Brandless. Useless. There was no way to prove this campsite belonged to the killer without a *Hey, it's me. I murdered that woman* sign, but what were the chances they had stumbled across a random site after descending Angel's Landing? "Based on the distance between the cliff and this campsite, I'd say we're on the right trail. He was here. Probably within the past couple of hours."

The weight of Branch's attention slid down her spine. He'd been watching her for a few minutes, whether he realized it or not. Any move she made seemed to intensify his presence, but she wasn't going to let him get to her again.

"Why wait?" Two words. That was enough.

She could practically feel the vibration of his voice across the empty space between them, as though he was standing within mere inches, which was nuts. Her mouth dried at the thought of all the other things he could say to her with that deep tone. Things he might whisper in the dark, tangled in her sheets with her secured against his unyielding chest.

Nope. Not happening. He'd made that perfectly clear. He didn't get close to people for a reason, and after he'd told her about his horrible experience with his ex, she didn't blame him. How did a person come back from something like that? From that kind of betrayal?

Blood drained from her face. Wait. What was his question again? "What do you mean?"

"The window of when Sarah Lantos died is between ten and two yesterday afternoon." Branch kicked at the ring of rocks that reigned in the embers still smoldering. "If this site belongs to the killer, why wait until this morning to flee? Why not get as far from the crime scene as possible while he could?"

Lila circled the campsite for the—she didn't know how many times—and followed the streaks carved into the dirt. Trying to cover his tracks? No. That didn't feel right. Not with the lack of treads in the killer's boots. Attempting to erase his presence would be redundant, and leaving a sandwich bag voided all that hard work.

But Branch had a point. Why stay here when rangers and the medical examiner's office would be all over the scene literally less than a half mile away? This clearing acted as a starting point that split into multiple escape routes through the valleys and backcountry trails. Maybe he hadn't meant to stay as long as he had.

Crouching beside one of the divots, she caught the pattern. Not with the treads but in the steps themselves. "Because he was injured."

Branch entered her peripheral vision, the scent she'd always attributed to him—cedar and something clean—driving into her system.

"See?" Guiding her finger over the nearest streak without disrupting the dirt, Lila ended at the empty boot print to the left. Then another streak, complete with a second boot print. Again to the left. Then a third.

"He wasn't trying to erase his tracks. His right leg is dragging behind his left." Branch took position beside her, only inches between them. One shift in her weight, and she'd get everything she'd craved in the past few months. It was as close as he'd ever voluntarily gotten, but Lila had to remind herself there was nothing personal about his proximity. He was simply trying to get a closer look at what she saw. "Would he have been able to scale Angel's Landing with an injury like this?"

"Depends on how old it is." That woodsy scent filled her, warmed her from the inside, and she breathed it in a bit deeper. If this was all she could have of Branch Thompson, she'd die a happy woman. Ugh, that sounded pathetic. Months of this crush must've warped her brain. "If it's a disability, he may have learned to compensate on his climbs over years of conditioning and training, but if it's recent, I don't see how."

"So it's possible Sarah Lantos could've fought back and injured her attacker." Why did Branch sound hopeful about that possibility? Like he wanted the killer to suffer for what he'd done? Deep lines etched between his brows as Branch seemed to memorize the tracks in front of them, and she wanted nothing more in that moment than to smooth them away. To offer him some kind of comfort.

He'd probably bite her hand off if she tried.

"Yeah. I guess it's possible." The breeze kicked up, cooling the sweat at her temples and increasing the intensity of cedar. Lila forced herself to stand, to get some distance on the pretense of searching the campsite for evidence when all she really wanted to do was clear her head of Branch. "Problem is we don't really know anything about her. Whether she was armed or capable of hurting him."

All they had was the driver's license attached to the permit Sarah Lantos had applied for to hike Angel's Landing. The license itself had been issued by the state of Washington and listed the woman's birthday and address, but that didn't mean that was where the victim had called home. The law enforcement division would take that information and run with it, but it didn't tell Lila if Sarah was married, if she had children, what she enjoyed in her down time or what kind of books she liked to read. She'd been a donor, but Lila couldn't imagine any of her organs helping someone else after a six-thousand-foot drop. As of right now, Sarah Lantos was only a body. A piece of a puzzle they had yet to figure out, and maybe that was what had sent Lila into two pints of Cherry Garcia last night after Risner dismissed her from the case.

Everyone needed someone on their side.

"How do you do it?" Branch kept his attention on the revealed pattern in the dirt. "See things the other rangers don't."

"Not sure what you mean, Grizzly Bear." Ice threaded through Lila's veins as she backed away from the treads. Not once in the four months, three weeks and two days Branch Thompson had set foot in Zion National Park had he ever asked her a personal question, and she wasn't entirely sure what to do with it now.

Branch straightened to his full height. That startling difference between them was enough to make her question every single daydream and fantasy she'd ever had. Not just physically. Mentally, emotionally.

Every move he made was calculated beforehand where she jumped at any opportunity that distracted her from the incessant thoughts in her head. He set out to push everyone away—to punish them or himself, she didn't know—when all she wanted was connection. Someone who surprised her with her favorite soda or brought her a cookie because they'd been thinking about her. Someone she could talk to, really talk to, without having to rely on death threats and sarcasm. Someone who knew all the bad but loved her anyway. In what world would a man like Branch choose to be with her?

"I worked homicides in Grand Canyon as a law enforcement ranger before coming to Zion. A lot of suicides, too." He stared out over the campsite. "It was an accident, really. Something I kind of fell into after the divorce four years ago. I didn't really know what to do with myself. I couldn't stay in the house we'd shared, couldn't see myself going back to work at a job she'd pushed me into for the income. Telling me it would be good for our family."

Every cell in Lila's body went still, as if one wrong move would break the spell of him opening up.

Branch scrubbed a hand down his face. "After I signed the papers, I found myself on the road, going from one park to the other, trying to figure out what came next. But standing in the middle of the most beautiful places on the planet, I felt... I just felt. For the first time in months, the anger, the hurt, the betrayal—none of it could get to me."

The half-hearted laugh that escaped his throat shocked her straight to the core. She'd never heard a more freeing sound and set a goal right then and there to make him laugh as much as possible. Just for the effect it had on releasing the tightness in her chest.

"I'd only been on the road a couple weeks, but I walked straight up to a ranger in Acadia National Park and asked how I could do his job. Within three months, I'd graduated the law enforcement training program, got my EMT certification, had a job with NPS and was assigned to work at the Grand Canyon." Turning, Branch set all that intensity on Lila, his expression unreadable but not as hard as she'd come to expect. "In my program, they taught you patrol procedures, enforcement operations, over a hundred hours of legal and behavioral science and firearms. Everything you need to protect people in the park, but even with all that training, NPS can't teach anyone how to pick up on the changes in your environment like you do.

That comes from years of being stuck in survival mode. Of being afraid."

Her throat threatened to close in on itself, and the mask she'd become so accustomed to wearing slipped. Leaving her as exposed as a raw nerve. She couldn't seem to force her brain to catch up, the shock holding her hostage.

"Who made you afraid, Lila?" His question didn't come with a lick of expectation or forcefulness but threatened to crack her open all the same.

"I'm not sure there's anything else we can get from this campsite, but if the killer's injury is fresh, we could catch up. He couldn't have got too much farther ahead in the past couple of hours." A tremor shook her hands, and she fisted her fingers to regain just a sliver of control.

Problem was, Branch always seemed to barrel through her ability to keep her head on straight. Lila headed for the man-size space between two bushes, the most logical path the killer had taken into the valley below. As long as she kept moving, she had a chance.

"And I know what you're thinking. It's presumptuous to assume the killer we're chasing identifies as male, but up to seventy percent of female homicide victims are killed by a male attacker, most of those by someone they knew before their deaths."

"Lila." Branch had no problem staying on her heels.

A rumble filtered through the panic clawing into her chest. Like thunder. Though there weren't many clouds in the sky. Keep moving. She just had to keep moving, and everything would be okay. And talking. And—

The rumble boiled into a full-blown roar, and she slowed.

"Lila!" Hard muscle slammed into her back.

Her feet left the ground. Strong arms locked around

her chest and hauled her closer to the mountain wall. Pain ignited down her side at the impact. "Branch—"

A shadow blocked out the sun, and a boulder exploded mere feet from her. Right where she'd been standing.

Chapter Ten

Heavy breathing punctured the ringing in his ears. Branch's lungs worked to discharge the dust he'd inhaled. It still danced in the air, clouding him and Lila in their own personal dirty snow globe.

The boulder that'd crashed to the earth mere feet away splintered down the middle. Chunks had broken off on impact, and it was all too easy to imagine the damage it would have caused had Branch not gotten them off the path.

His fingers protested as he loosened his grip on her arms. Damn, he'd held onto her tight enough, he was sure he'd left bruises on her flawless, sun-kissed skin. "Talk to me."

Her coughs vibrated through her pack into his chest. Jerky and irregular. "I'm alive. You can let go of me."

Right. The danger had passed—as far as he knew. So why did it take so much effort to command his hands to let go? Branch peeled his body from hers one inch at a time, instantly aware of the loss of her warmth.

Rockfalls were the most common natural disasters within the parks, but this was his first. Any number of geologic processes contributed to them: weathering, bedrock fractures, earthquakes, erosion. There was no predicting the outcome, and he sure as hell wasn't looking forward to a repeat. If he hadn't noticed the few smaller rocks tumbling down the cliff before that boulder had followed...

No. He didn't want to think about that. Didn't want to consider what would've happened to Lila if he'd let her take one more step.

Lila slapped a hand against the towering cliff face, bracing herself as she brought that sky blue gaze to his. Then she glanced at the pieces of rock that could've crushed her more thoroughly than Sarah Lantos's fall from Angel's Landing. Her face paled. "Thank you."

Shaky but confident. And he was still coiled tight as a spring. Branch didn't trust himself to speak as adrenaline kept its restrictive vice around his heart, nodding instead.

The change was slow this time, as if Lila had forgotten her armor had dropped. Dirt trickled down the rock face under her touch. Then she brought her hand to her head and shoved that practiced smile in place. "If you wanted a reason to touch me, Ranger Thompson, all you had to do was ask."

"You sign legal documents in glitter pen, don't you?" He hated his title and last name coming out of her sweet mouth. Well, as sweet as it could be with death threats every few minutes. Turned out, he kind of liked them. Her playfulness and creativity. Her unwavering determination to make him as uncomfortable as possible in her own way. As much as he hated the idea of letting anyone get under his skin, Lila had a true talent for tricking his defenses into letting her slide on in. Branch couldn't deny the electricity in his veins in the few minutes since they'd escaped death.

"And use pinky promises as a foundation of trust." She

winked at him with a twist of her mouth. Showcasing the laceration at her temple. "Shall we find a killer then?"

"You're bleeding." Every cell in his body screamed at him in condemnation. He'd done this. Used too much force and failed to protect her head when he'd practically tackled her against the rock wall.

Branch caught her arm before she had a chance to run from him, spinning her into his chest. Her palm pressed over his heart. Even with their height differences—she was more than a foot shorter than him—she fit against him perfectly. The perfect little murderous creature he hadn't been able to ignore no matter how many times he tried. He prodded at the cut with the pad of his thumb, careful not to inflict more damage.

Lila flinched under the invasion. Or maybe the adrenaline had finally evened out, and her body got the message that something was wrong. "Ow."

"Sorry." Blood was already crusting at the edges. She wouldn't have to worry about stitches. "The cut isn't deep, but we should clean it to avoid infection."

Her breath tickled the underside of his jaw as she looked up at him. "Okay."

It took more energy than he expected to back away from the press of her body against his. Maneuvering his pack to his front, Branch dug for his first aid kit and laid it out on the ground between them. Alcohol prep pads and his water would do the best job of killing bacteria and flushing debris from the wound. "This might hurt."

"Haven't you heard? Barbies don't feel pain." Streaks of dirt interrupted the smooth skin of her cheek and forehead, sharpening her features to an almost ethereal level. Lila Jordan was breathtakingly beautiful, though he'd just started allowing himself to see past that first layer of defense to the trapped woman beneath.

"You know about that?" Branch focused on cleaning blood from the laceration in small sections. Overall the cut wasn't more than two inches long, but the jagged pieces of skin at the edges made it difficult to ensure Lila didn't walk out of this park worse off than when she started. She took his ministrations like a champ, though.

"You mean what the other rangers say about me? That I'm an airhead, and I only care about my looks? Oooh, how about that I throw temper tantrums if I don't get the shifts I want? I'm shallow and clingy, and I don't take anything seriously. I use my assets to manipulate my superiors, and I was handed this job by performing sexual favors. Yeah. I know about that."

The brightness in her eyes dimmed, and Branch couldn't help but free the anger he'd relied on to get him into this new stage of life. At the hurt in those blue depths. She'd known exactly how their coworkers—how Risner—perceived her, and yet, from his observations, she hadn't done anything to earn their judgment. He'd simply gone with the flow. Never joining in conversations centered around her, but he hadn't done anything to shut them down, either, and he hated himself for it.

"I know I can come on a bit strong." She shrugged. "I know what they all call me and how everyone tries to get out of working shifts with me. I ask too many personal questions. Sometimes it turns people off when I want to know what's going on in their lives, but I only ever wanted them to feel like they had a friend. You know? Someone they could talk to on breaks or meet for a movie. Come to if they needed help. Working on the trails can get lonely. I just wanted to help make it a little more bearable, but they don't need me, and that's okay. Talking behind my back and making up nicknames helps them bond with each other, and who am I to get in the way of that?"

She had to be joking. Lila had to see the damage that had been done by letting people disrespect and devalue her.

He couldn't stop a torrent of memories from the past few months. Her throwing surprise birthday parties for the other rangers in the headquarters break room, complete with balloons of their favorite color and cake of their favorite flavor. Her handing out gift cards from local restaurants with an invite to get together for lunch. The dozens of times she'd brought her coworkers coffee at the start of her shift, including him.

Branch finished cleaning the cut, taping a butterfly bandage in place. Realization hit. She hadn't done any of it for them. Hell, Ranger Barbie was...lonely. "That first time we worked together. You asked me out to coffee after our shift, and I turned you down."

"Not sure a growl counts as a rejection, but you got your point across." She pressed her pink manicured fingertips over the bandage with a half smile of appreciation. "The rangers here have worked together for years. They're part of each other's lives. I just wanted to help you fit in, but I don't hold it against you, not wanting to get coffee or have me show you around Springdale. I'm not everyone's cup of tea."

But she wanted to be. He could hear it in her voice. Saw it in the slip of her smiles. Smiles he was sure covered a pain she hadn't let anyone glimpse, and Branch couldn't let it go. The idea that her detailed perception in this case had been born of someone who had made her afraid, cultivated due to long periods of time spent in her fight, flight or freeze response. It was a coping mechanism of trauma survivors forced to adapt—to anticipate—a threat before it occurred in the name of protecting themselves.

He wanted nothing more than to wipe the face of the earth free of whatever threat she was running from. While he'd gone out of his way to isolate himself from everyone around him to endure the pain he'd suffered, Lila had never chosen to become an outcast.

Blond hair escaped from her low ponytail beneath her Stetson, and Branch shot a hand out to swipe it back behind her ear.

An indescribable need to ease that dullness in her gaze and fight her battles took hold. "I'm not a fan of tea, but I'm open to recommendations. If your invitation still stands."

Her mouth parted, and the loss of all those defenses she'd kept in place only made her more beautiful. Real. This…this was the woman he'd caught glimpses of under the mask. And, damn, he'd never seen a more perfect sight. She was still holding back, but he could be patient. He had nowhere else to be.

"Sure." That single answer left her mouth as more breath than coherent word, gifting him the slightest hint at what she might sound like pinned beneath him, his mouth on her skin, his hands tangled in her hair.

A swirl of desire caught him by surprise, nearly knocking him off-balance. Shit. He hadn't felt anything close to this since before his divorce, but Lila had somehow made it easy. Constantly presenting a mystery to solve.

Branch ordered his hand to drop away from her face and his feet to add a few inches between them before he did something neither of them were prepared for. "We should keep moving in case there are more boulders looking to relocate."

"Right." Lila shook her head as though he'd affected her concentration.

Couldn't say he was sorry, either. Turnabout was fair play.

"This valley separates into three different canyons. The killer could've taken any one of them to put as much distance between him and the crime scene, but the most passable is the one heading north." Lila took a step in that direction. "I'm betting if he didn't bother covering his tracks at the campsite, he didn't take the time to make sure we couldn't follow."

The analytical part of his brain—influenced by his training and experience in two different national parks—attacked the heat simmering in his gut and shut it down. He'd only ever reviewed these canyons on a map. He'd have to rely on Lila's knowledge of the area moving forward. "How far north can he get?"

"About forty miles. It wouldn't be difficult. That canyon has seen some flooding, but we're far enough into the summer months most of it would've cleared." Pointing out over the valley, she targeted their next destination. "All he'd have to do is follow the river as far north as possible before he can disappear into wilderness."

"And get away with murder." Branch wasn't going to let that happen. They'd packed light. Certainly not with enough supplies to spend days in the wilderness, but the sooner they caught up with the killer, the sooner he could try that cup of tea. "We need to get to check in with Risner. You okay to pick up the—"

An explosion rocked through the mountain above. Rock spewed in every direction and arched through the sky, and both he and Lila threw their arms overhead to block the debris. In vain. Vibrations shook up his legs as torrents of dirt blocked out the sun. Growing louder. Closer.

"Landslide." Branch shoved his partner ahead of him as the first sheets of dirt rained down. "Run!"

Chapter Eleven

Pain. She couldn't breathe, couldn't think. It felt as though a boulder was sitting on her chest. Or she'd been body-slammed again.

It had all happened so fast: the shaking; Branch's order for her to run; the darkness. She hadn't made it more than few steps before the first rock had knocked her to the ground.

Had it been an earthquake? Zion was positioned near four minor fault lines, but nothing had triggered anything like this in the past. That first boulder could've been a warning.

Exhaustion urged Lila to slip back into unconsciousness—to take away the pain—but there was something she had to do. A reason why she was here. Why couldn't she remember?

Dust caught in her throat, and her body jerked to dispel the invasion. Once. Twice. Searing pain shot through her side as she tried to roll onto her stomach. She couldn't stop the moan scraping up her dry throat. Everything hurt, and she was dying. Curling her fingernails into the ground, she fisted a handful of what felt like gravel.

Dirt slipped into her uniform and rubbed in all the wrong ways. She pressed one hand into her ribs, prying open gritty eyes. Meeting nothing but darkness. The moan contorted into a whimper as she tried to take a full breath. Her ribs screamed in protest, only allowing shaky, shallow inhales. "H-hello? Can...anyone hear me?"

No answer.

At least not any that she could hear. Sunlight filtered in from above, helping her eyes adjust to the unstable walls threatening to crush her. "Branch?"

Where was he? Was he hurt? The taste of copper filled her mouth. She swiped at it, coming away with something sticky and warm, but she couldn't make it out clearly enough. Blood?

Lila studied the precarious positions of the boulders overhead. One wrong move, and the entire house of cards could come down on her. It was a miracle it hadn't already. Sand trickled between the cracks and stole some of the sunlight, which felt like death in and of itself when she imagined being stuck without a way to see. Being truly alone. Forgotten. She swallowed past the thin coating of dirt in her mouth. Her bottom lip wavered with a held sob. She could do this. She had to do this.

"Help."

Her call barely filled the too small space in which she'd been thrown. No. Shoved. Branch had shoved her ahead of him. He'd saved her life. Again. The sob built in her chest until it consumed what little air she'd managed to hold onto. It was only a matter of time before this dark little hole collapsed or was filled with dirt. She couldn't be here for that. She had to get out.

"Branch!"

Lightning speared through her side and behind her eyes. Tears burned down her face. Every NPS ranger was required to earn their EMT certification. She was trained to remain calm in case of emergency and to assess any potential injuries. Breathe. She just had to breathe. One breath. Two. Both hurt like a mother, but prodding her fingers along the epicenter of the pain in her side, she concluded her ribs weren't broken or cracked. Most likely bruised. She'd live.

Hopefully not in this hole.

"Okay. Step one—don't panic. Easier said than done. Whoever came up with that step clearly wasn't buried under a mountain." Lila swiped at her face, caking dirt and tears to her hands. Focus. There had to be a way out of here, to get to Branch. Make sure he was alive. One step at a time. That was all she could do.

"Step two—assess for injuries." Inventorying the rest of her body, she was grateful to find nothing but a few cuts and bruises in the low light coming through the cracks. A gash cut across her shin, but it was difficult to see the damage clearly.

Working her pack from her shoulders with nothing less than four moans and one scream, she dragged it to her chest and searched for her first aid kit, flashlight and a bottle of water. Three large boulders had pinned her in place, with the largest overhead. Any movement against them and she was dead. One wrong move? Dead. Another earthquake? Dead. Which only made escape that much harder. Great.

She curled her upper body off the ground, holding onto her ribs to contain the gut-nauseating spike in pain and unpacked her kit. "Step three—don't die of infection."

Alcohol pads, a little water from her bottle, her largest bandage and a few tabs of ibuprofen did the job.

"Four—figure out where the hell you are." She hit the power button on her flashlight. She had about three feet of space overhead, a few more to her right and only a foot or so to her left. Smaller rocks acted as nothing but annoyances. It was the big ones she'd have to watch out for. Though how she was going to chest press a two-ton boulder was beyond her. She regularly hit the weights—even managed a PR last week—but this felt a little out of her reach. "Well, it could use some color, but otherwise, not so bad."

Who was she kidding? This place was a hole. Almost literally. But she hadn't cried in a few minutes. She'd count that as a win. Lila shifted onto her stomach, searching for... Okay. She didn't know. Something, anything, that might look like a Jenga piece she could pull without setting the whole tower down on top of her? Dirt grated against her skin beneath today's kerchief as she toed herself closer to the wall of rock ahead. A collection of smaller boulders—the size of basketballs—were wedged tight. The mammoth rock hanging over her head was supported by these smaller ones on this side of the death trap. "Okay. So you guys are off-limits."

Craning the flashlight to her right, she lost count of the number of rocks squeezed into every nook and cranny between two of the largest boulders. Those could work. They were higher off the ground. Very little chance of causing a complete collapse with the larger boulder ready to take the weight. Where was her architectural engineer dad when she needed him?

She stopped that thought in its tracks. She didn't need him. She'd been doing just fine on her own.

More than fine. Maybe a little lonely with no one but a roommate she barely saw once a week—if she was lucky. Her parents and siblings blamed her for the destruction of the family and wanted nothing to do with her, but she had a good job. She got to work in one of the most beautiful places in the world.

Though getting trapped underneath it wasn't great.

She could get a little obsessed with romantic comedies and probably went overboard on the Ben & Jerry's more than she wanted to admit. Her boss and fellow rangers avoided her at all costs, mimicking and mocking her when they thought she wasn't paying attention. Oh, and then there was her unhealthy crush on a man who would never see her as anything more than a coworker because of his whole messed-up past and bad attitude, but damn it, she was fine.

Where was Branch? Had he survived? Was he hurt? She wouldn't let herself believe anything worse.

The fact was no one was coming to save her. If she was being honest with herself, nobody cared she was out here, about to die, and wasn't that a kick while she was down? Risner would pretend to grieve but ultimately just want to get himself some attention. There would be a service. She could see him now, giving some big speech where he went out of his way to tell people how close they were. The sexist asshole.

Sayles might shed a few tears, but she'd have her big, strong FBI agent boyfriend to help her through it. The other rangers would probably use the gift cards she'd given them to go out together. Her family considered her dead a long time ago. And Branch… Her heart tried to tell her he wasn't all grizzly bear and growls, but they didn't know each other. Nobody really knew her. Which meant, even if she got out of here, she had nothing to go back to. No one.

Gravity intensified its hold on her body. Trying to bury her in all the bad feelings. But she had her smile. She had those little pockets of happiness, even if it came bottled from the pharmacy.

"I'm not as mean as I could be, and people should be more grateful for that." Lila got her knees under her, her head bumping the ceiling of her little cave. If she weren't about to die, this would be a great shelter in the middle of a storm, but she wasn't planning on sticking around to test that theory. Her injured ribs squeezed, and she lost the air from her lungs. Another moan slipped free, but she used the pain to keep her in the moment. To focus on reaching for that first rock. "Just like playing Jenga. Nothing to it."

She didn't even believe herself. The rock—about the size of her hand—came quietly, and Lila released the tension she'd held in her neck. "See? Nothing."

The boulder overhead shuddered. Then sank another couple inches.

Her scream triggered ringing in her own ears as she flattened herself against the ground. Dust settled, a few other rocks came loose. And she waited to die with her eyes pinched tight.

Except she wasn't dead yet. Her lungs seemed to get the message, letting go of the need to hyperventilate. She pried her eyes open. Instantly blinded by the increased sliver of sunlight coming from between the two largest boulders. It wasn't much. Definitely not enough for her to crawl through, but a couple more rocks might fix that. "Please, just let me have the chance to kiss Branch before I die."

That was all she wanted. All she'd ever wanted. And if he was out there—hurt, alone—she had to get to him.

She collected the flashlight she'd dropped and shoved it in her pack before threading her arms through the straps. One shot. She had to make it a good one. Lila two-handed a basketball-size boulder and put her weight into dislodging it from its position. The rock tumbled free, landing short of her kneecaps. She pumped her fist gently up at the boulder threatening to end her puny existence. "Yay me."

The next part would be the trickiest. *Tricky. Tricky. Tricky.* Nope. She had to down the urge to start singing Run-D.M.C. Those would not be her last words if this went poorly.

A few other rocks skittered down the slope wedged between the two boulders, but she'd managed to clear a good amount. The breeze trickled into the cave-slash-prison, and for the first time since waking, she could really breathe. For now. She could see trees and mountains and sky. And dirt. An entire waterfall of dirt.

Was Branch out there? Was he looking for her? Was he as worried about her as she was for him?

Grabbing for the next section of rock, Lila set each down peacefully in an attempt to not anger the earth gods. She could do this. Excruciating seconds turned into excruciating minutes as she carefully removed and set down each piece of the very dangerous puzzle.

Finally, a hole large enough she could fit through held strong. Another sob built in her throat, but she swallowed it back. She could have a mental breakdown after she got the hell out of here. Preferably in the shower. With ice cream. And one of her favorite scream-o songs on repeat. Everyone needed a self-care day.

She unshouldered her pack and tossed it through the opening. If she didn't make it out of this, at least someone would know where she'd met her maker. No time to think. She just had to move.

Lila thrust herself through the opening. The ledge of rock under her ribs gave out, and she sank a couple of inches. The next scream was lost on a gust of wind as panic took control. Clawing her nails into the dirt, she shoved through as the boulder shifted down with a rumble. Her toes cleared the deathtrap, and Lila collapsed onto her back.

"Well, aren't you a determined little thing?" The outline of a man cast a shadow over her from above, though she could make out his features as her vision darkened. Strong hands wrapped around her arms. "Looks like you're coming with me."

Chapter Twelve

Drip. Drip. Drip.

Branch cracked his eyes open to an upside-down world. His head thudded hard. Something sticky and...wrong plastered against his face. He swiped at it. Blood seeped into the loops and whorls of his finger pads. He followed the drops to a rock below, the source of the soft ticking that'd brought him around. The headache hit then, strong and disorienting. He closed his eyes against the dizziness, but it was no use as long as he was strung up like a piñata.

His pack pulled at his shoulders, swinging above—or was it below?—his head. He tucked his chin to his chest to get a better look at what kept him from splatting against the rocks at the base of the tree. His boot had caught between two bare branches, but his heel was already sliding free from his shoe. A fifteen-foot drop wouldn't work in his favor. Hell.

The landslide had come out of nowhere. He remembered shoving Lila ahead of him to make sure she cleared most of the rock, but...he didn't remember much after that.

Lila.

Scanning the dirt and rock beneath him for anything coming close to pink, Branch felt the uptick in his heart rate. She had to be here. She had to be okay. He swung his arms out like a starfish, and his boot slid another few centimeters. There was only one way he was getting out of this alive.

He slipped his pack free and let it drop. His supplies hit the ground with a too loud thud that triggered another sharp spear of pain in his skull. Curling his upper body, he grabbed for the branch that'd saved his life. And missed. Every muscle in his torso protested the smallest movement. Oxygen crushed from his lungs. He straightened back out to regain his breath, and his boot took the opportunity to remind him he'd run out of time. A drop from this height promised a slow death if he managed to protect his head. Not an outcome he was looking forward to. "Come on."

Branch curled again. His fingertips brushed the rough tree bark but ultimately failed to grasp hold. The momentum and weight of his body pulled his heel free of his boot, and he shot up one last time. Bark cut through the calloused skin of his palm as he gripped the branch. His legs lost the battle to gravity, and he hung upright above the sloped landscape. With his boot still stuck in the tree. He stared up at it, out of reach. "Traitor."

Though he had to acknowledge he wasn't about to die. Gauging the distance between him and the ground, he took the chance. His stomach shot into his throat a split second before he hit the dirt, rolling to avoid breaking his unsupported ankle. Dirt clung to every inch of his body, worked beneath his clothes. Irritated...places.

Scrubbing a hand down his face, Branch fell against the tree's trunk for support. Shit. How long had he been hanging there draining like a slaughtered cow?

His vision wavered, and Branch grabbed for his pack,

sinking to the ground. He had to stop the bleeding. Head wounds usually bled more due to the amount and location of blood vessels, but he couldn't determine how deep the wound was without cleaning it first. His mouth dried as he caught sight of his water bottle, and he took a few pulls to stay hydrated. It would be all too easy to get dehydrated out here in the middle of nowhere in over one-hundred-degree heat. He couldn't do a damn thing for Lila if he wasn't taking care of himself.

Washing the wound and his face with a couple handfuls of water, he set about cleaning the injury with the last remaining alcohol pad in his kit. He didn't have a mirror, no way of telling if he needed stitches, so a larger butterfly bandage would have to do. The same he'd used for Lila after that first boulder had tried to kill them.

He should've taken it for the sign it was. Branch studied the devastation of the landscape around him. Fifty-foot trees had been half buried. Boulders that'd outlasted hundreds of years of storms cracked open around him. Dead logs and dirt had swept through and obliterated everything within a quarter mile.

Landslides weren't uncommon in Zion. A couple of the most popular trails had been closed down in the past few months due to shifting, but he'd never seen anything like this.

He hadn't heard it, either, that telltale roar that sounded the alarm in an event like this. But there had been an explosion...

Branch shoved a protein bar in his mouth to combat the fatigue flooding through him and hauled his pack to his back. Lila was out here. Alone, possibly injured. He had to move fast. The woman wasn't the type to sit around and wait for someone to rescue her.

Despite her innocent facade and obsession with the color pink, there was something vicious and unpredictable beneath that smile. He'd glimpsed it only a couple times—mostly when she was threatening him—but Lila would go out of her way to prove she didn't need anyone but herself. Potentially hurting herself in the process despite her training and familiarity with the area.

They had that in common. While he could pinpoint the moment in his life when he'd cut himself off from the world and convinced himself he was better off alone, Lila kept that part of her life to herself. There was no telling how far she'd push herself to survive. Better he found her before it came to that.

His muscles burned as he hauled himself up the incline to where the landslide had started, leaving his boot behind. The trail they'd been following was gone, buried under several tons of rock and dirt and trees. The landslide hadn't started with a trickle. It'd come in an explosion of death and destruction, suddenly and violently. From this angle, Branch could just make out the jagged shards where the mountain had been carved apart. Too straight. Too sharp. It looked almost…intentional.

Didn't matter right now. Sucking in deep breaths from where the landslide impacted the trail, he surveyed the scope of the damage. At least a quarter mile of the valley was lost. Had Lila survived it?

Pain that had nothing to do with getting thrown around like a rag doll took up residence in his chest. Branch rubbed his bloodied hand into his sternum to try to ease the pressure, but it was no use. He hadn't known. That meddling little banshee had worked her way into his life over the past couple of days. Now she was just…gone? No way in hell was he giving up.

Reaching for his radio, he hit nothing but an empty belt. Damn it. It must've detached during the landslide. Two other teams had set out to track this killer, each expected to check in regularly with updates, but how long would Risner wait before suspecting he and Lila were in trouble? Hours? Days? Knowing the district ranger's hostile relationship with Lila, he'd wait until nightfall, rooting for another team to contribute something worthwhile to the investigation.

Maneuvering his pack to his front, Branch unpacked his cell phone from the front pocket. The screen had cracked from his tumble down the mountain, but the device itself still had battery life. But no service bars. He'd have to hike out of the valley to get a signal. He tossed the phone back into his pack. "This day keeps getting better and better."

What he wouldn't give for one of Lila's death threats now. Just to hear her voice. To absorb a bit of her overzealous enthusiasm. She'd list all the ways they were lucky to be alive and try to recruit him into starting a gratitude journal. Which he would do without her knowledge. Just as he'd bought himself a pint of Cherry Garcia after watching her drop an armload into her cart at the only grocery store in Springdale a few weeks ago. And streamed her favorite romantic comedy after she'd referenced it in the break room a month before that.

He didn't know what it was about her erratic daydreaming heart that had caught his attention the second he stepped into Zion. Everything she was—impulsive, emotional, upbeat—defined everything he wasn't, but he couldn't seem to let go. If anything, she'd hooked him deeper over these past couple of days, and he didn't hate it. He'd come to crave her promises of murder and learning about her expertise in everything ranging from ballet to calligraphy.

Following the upper ridge of the landslide, he gritted against the small punctures of rocks biting into his socked foot. Dust puffed off his clothing with every step, the sun only making the pounding in his head worse. "Lila!"

His shout echoed off the cliff faces standing as sentries around the valley below. But there was no other response.

No glimpse of pink.

No sign she'd survived.

His chest tightened against the possibility of never setting sight on that hot pink manicure she protected with the fierceness of a pit bull. Or watching her guard drop when she thought no one was looking. And he wasn't leaving until he found her.

Tossing his pack to the ground, Branch mapped the most likely place she would have succumbed to the landslide, probably a few hundred feet down from their original position on the trail. His heels sank into loose earth, threatening to pull him under as he descended. "I'm coming, Barbie. Don't give up."

Larger boulders took shape at the bottom of the incline. There was too much ground to cover in the search, and randomly digging would only waste time Lila might not have. He needed a narrower search grid. He needed a clue to her location. "Lila!"

Again, no answer. The anger he'd managed to suppress since this morning reared its ugly head, but with it came a whole new slew of emotions determined to knock him on his ass. Hopelessness. Abandonment. The things he'd nearly lost his fight to after the divorce. It hadn't just been about losing a woman he'd loved for more than fifteen years. He'd lost a future. A best friend. Everything he'd cared about because of the misdirected impulsiveness of a single person.

Maybe that was why he'd avoided Lila for so long, convinced that having any kind of relationship with her would only end up killing him all over again. Why he'd offered favors to switch shifts, turned down her attempts at getting to know each other and sat as far from her as possible in any team meeting. In the end, he'd treated her as everyone else had. Disposable. Overlooked. Unimportant. And, damn it, she deserved better.

Lila wasn't his ex. And he sure as hell wasn't going to lose her. Not like this.

Branch scoured the site, every cell in his body focused on picking out something—anything—that didn't belong. He just needed a starting point. A pink kerchief. A manicured hand. Hot pink boot laces.

Sun glinted off a metallic surface. No. Not metallic. A bejeweled backpack.

His lungs emptied a split second before he dashed down the incline, toward the boulders at the bottom of the hill. Heart threatening to beat through his rib cage, Branch skidded into the pack as though he was rounding home base and clutched the canvas to his chest. It was hers. But Lila...

"Where are you?" Scanning the area, he noted the body-size hole between boulders with a few scattered stones along the ground. As though someone had crawled free of a grave.

A quick inspection told him she wasn't inside. She wasn't here at all. She wouldn't have left her pack voluntarily.

Branch took another look at the dirt around the boulder. Picking up on a second set of prints. No treads. With a drag mark to the right. The same boot prints they'd found at the campsite.

Ice coursed through his veins. Lila hadn't walked away from the landslide.

She'd been taken.

Chapter Thirteen

Her moan pulled her back into consciousness. Or had she been snoring? It was hard to tell.

Pine branches swayed above her, glimpses of sunlight bearing down in between them. The ground was soft beneath her. And sweaty. Like lying on a sleeping bag.

That wasn't right. Last she'd checked, she was about to be squashed like a pancake by a boulder twenty times her size. And then… She couldn't remember anything else.

"You're awake." The voice came from somewhere to her right. Deep and vibrating. Almost…amused? Movement out of the corner of her eye convinced her brain to burn the last of the haze. The owner's outline grew larger as he drew close. Dragging one foot behind the other. "I was beginning to think I wouldn't have any use for you after all, Ranger Jordan."

Oh. Damn it. She'd been kidnapped.

Shadows played across a deeply tanned face as a new gust of wind startled the tree overhead. Dark brows cut across a broad forehead lined with age markers. Midforties at least. Salt peppered through a few days of beard growth and at the temples of dark hair. His eyes were a bit sunken, surrounded by fine lines, but his face overall was soft. Bands of muscle fought to break free of the tight long-sleeved shirt he wore. Polyester if she had to guess, wicking, quick-drying. Something a seasoned climber might use, along with the loose nylon pants currently covered in blood.

It took a minute for her name to register. Then she remembered her uniform came complete with a name tag to make it easier for hikers and visitors to verbally abuse her on the trails. Seemed the landslide hadn't deemed it worth destroying.

Lila rolled to her side, instantly reminded of the bruises across her rib cage. The pain struck as though she'd been kicked in the gut as she settled her weight on all fours over a sleeping bag that most definitely wasn't hers. "I don't know you."

"But I know you." Tipping the point of a pocketknife in her direction, the man she assumed to be Sarah Lantos's killer settled against the trunk of the tree a few feet away. "I know you're the one who's leading the charge to find me. You discovered Sarah's body. You were the one who tested my climbing gear. The one leading your partner straight to me."

Had he been watching her? Creepy. And definitely the killer.

"Where is Branch?" Her chest hurt. She was thirsty, and her stomach felt as though it'd started eating itself. Or maybe she'd developed an ulcer in the past couple hours. Anything was possible.

Searching what looked like a smaller campsite than the one they'd come across earlier, Lila cataloged whatever was in sight. And what wasn't, her pack included. She'd tossed it, trying to let any search-and-rescue rangers know her location, but did they even realize what'd happened? The US Geological Survey monitored every national park for seismic activity. Did a landslide qualify? Would SAR be deployed in time to recover Branch?

"The last I saw of him, he was getting swept away with a whole bunch of dirt." He enunciated a low whistle with a flutter of his fingertips, clutching an apple and the pocketknife in the other hand. Very Bond villain, if she was being honest. All he needed was a white cat to stroke as he revealed all his evil plans. "Can't imagine he survived. Dynamite can be very unpredictable. You're very lucky you're still alive. For a moment there I thought you were a goner with all those boulders. By the way, how did you survive?"

Dynamite? Her heart shot into her throat. No. Branch was still alive. He had to be. Because the alternative...

Lila kept her gaze on the weapon in the man's hand. To give herself something to focus on other than the heartbreak threatening to claw her apart from the inside. "You caused the landslide. You killed—"

"Yes, yes. I'm the bad guy. I killed Sarah Lantos and shoved her over the side of Angel's Landing. I killed your partner. I destroyed part of your precious park. Blah, blah, blah." Leaning forward, her kidnapper waved a hand.

Tears burned in her eyes, though she honestly doubted she'd drunk enough to provide much release. Her kidnapper had brought her deeper into the valley. Flat landscape surrounded this little pine oasis, making her nothing but a target if she ran. The only other option was sprinting for the canyons, but without her supplies, she wouldn't last more than a day. Maybe two. "What do you want?"

"I have a problem." He limped toward her, heavily relying on his uninjured leg. Cutting along the seam of his pant leg, the killer exposed the bloody wound in his thigh. "And you're going to fix it."

"She stabbed you." Branch had been right about the victim fighting off her attacker before she'd gone over the edge of the cliff. He'd probably rub it in her face for days if he found out. "Sarah Lantos. She fought back."

"Not before I stabbed her first." The corner of his mouth quirked to one side, and Lila's stomach rolled. It was nothing compared to the slight twitches of Branch's mouth that told her he found her amusing if not a little exhausting. This one was completely acidic.

She shook her head, forcing her gaze to the killer's face. Memorizing everything she could about it. Though now that she thought about it, he'd probably planned on killing her to make sure she couldn't identify him. Still, hostage or not, sometimes it was nice to be held. "I don't have my first aid kit."

"Then it's a good thing I came prepared with more than a pocketknife." Adjusting his weight, he took a seat on the ground alongside her, his injured leg nearly touching her hip.

She could run. Based on the amount of blood oozing from the injury at the back of his thigh, he probably wouldn't be able to catch her. Then again, he'd obviously been able to stay conscious and alive since stabbing Sarah Lantos yesterday afternoon and managed to drag her to this campsite, so there was a chance she'd only be making her situation worse.

The weight of his attention curdled the coffee she'd substituted for breakfast this morning. "I will catch you, Ranger Jordan, and I won't be as careful with you as I was bringing you here."

One second. Two. She raised her gaze to his, shutting down the shiver working to break free up her spine.

"Get the kit." He nodded toward a pack at the end of the sleeping bag she'd woken on. "Front enclosure."

Her hands shook as she followed instructions. She couldn't seem to get the zipper around the curve of the pack as she searched for the easiest route to run long distance. Years of traversing these trails had blessed her with muscles she couldn't name. She had no doubt she'd be able to outrun this guy on a good day, but that meant leaving Branch behind. Possibly injured.

She got the zipper unfastened and freed the first aid kit inside. This was why she'd petitioned rangers outside of the law enforcement division to carry weapons, but Risner had shut that down real fast. Accusing her of most likely injuring herself with a Taser rather than her intended target. When she got back to headquarters, she'd show him exactly how accurate her aim was for putting her in this position.

Lila made a show of zipping the front enclosure with one hand while prying the larger compartment open. A gun stared back at her. Sitting right on top. She couldn't tamp down the shudder shaking across her shoulders as she shoved it deeper into the pack. Just in case. Crossing the sleeping bag, she settled the first aid kit in front of her and popped the lid. "You got a name?"

His laugh practically took physical shape between them. "Why are you asking?"

"Because saying, 'Hey, asshole, this is going to hurt' is awkward." Tearing a slit up the side of his pants, she exposed the wound farther. Blood crusted around the edges, but whatever his victim had done hit deep, most likely nicking a major vein. He was still bleeding from an injury he couldn't reach at the back of his thigh, and if she didn't irrigate and clean the wound, he would suffer from infection and greater blood loss. Not enough to kill him, though. At least, not soon enough.

"You don't need my name." He flinched at her touch. Baby. She hadn't even started cleaning the wound yet.

"Fine. Then I will assign one for you." She used the gauze pads to scrub as much blood from the edges as possible, using his water to break up the flakes. She tucked the water bottle between her thighs for easy access when the time came. She wasn't trying to be careful or mindful of his pain. In fact, she wanted this to hurt as much as possible, but other than that first flinch, the killer didn't seem to feel anything. Had he felt anything when he'd killed Sarah Lantos? Lila put as much hatred into her expression as possible as she leveled her gaze with his and dug her nails into the sides of the wound. "I'm going to call you Covid. For obvious reasons."

Another laugh startled her. This one had more bite, and it stuck in her body and refused to get the hell out. The smile that contorted his face fell, and before she had a chance to react, the killer crushed his hand against her throat. And squeezed.

"You make jokes to distract yourself from what hurts. All of these additions to your uniform, the pink nails, the makeup, the bleached hair. Everything I see about you makes me think you work so hard to make the outside beautiful because the inside is rotten. What was it, Ranger Jordan? Mommy didn't love you enough? Daddy hit you a little too often? Or was it something much, much more terrifying?"

Air lodged in her chest, and her defenses automatically had her reaching for his wrist to break the hold.

But he wouldn't budge. Panic flared, rolling through her and clenching every muscle she owned. He was so much bigger than she was. So much stronger. The pocketknife he'd held was right there. Her gaze darted down to it, then back up so as not to give herself away, but she was getting desperate. For air. For escape. For him to stop.

The killer dragged her upper body over his leg, close enough she could smell the sweetness of the apple he'd been eating on his breath. He scanned her from scalp to chin, those dark eyes seemingly undoing years of defenses. Loosening his hold, he let his fingers brush beneath the kerchief at her neck. Then untied the knot. The fabric fell away easily, exposing her—and the scar beneath—to him in a way she'd never allowed for anyone.

"You want people to take you seriously, but you keep them at arm's length. You hide from them. Lie to them. Like a magician, you keep their attention on one thing while the trick is happening in another place altogether."

"Everybody needs a hobby." Lila tried to pull back, to put those precious inches back between them, but he'd locked his hand around her throat a second time. That unreadable expression focused solely on the marred skin across her neck. Her pulse thudded—too hard—against his hand.

"Tell me who did this to you." His thumb pressed into the scar tissue spanning straight over her throat.

Her training failed her in every regard. She didn't know what to do, what to think about his request. So similar to the one Branch had made of her. *Who made you afraid?*

Lila slid one hand around the metal water bottle she'd used to clean the killer's wound. Then bashed it as hard as she could into his face. His groan punctured through the haze he'd created. The grip at her throat vanished, and she shoved to stand.

Lila ran toward the canyon mouth, unwilling to look back. And hoped she came out on the other side alive.

Chapter Fourteen

There was no other sign of her. The drag marks Branch had noted ended at a section of cascading boulders leading down into the valley. Even from this vantage point, it felt as though Lila had simply disappeared.

The killer couldn't have taken her far. Not with the injury he and Lila suspected he'd sustained, but if they'd been wrong—if the killer had trained and compensated around a disability—Branch feared he might never find her.

But why take Lila in the first place? The killer hadn't gone through her supplies as far as Branch could tell. Which meant he'd needed her for something. But what? And for how long?

His entire body ached with unchecked bruises, muscle strain and exhaustion as he navigated the maze of boulders leading down in the valley. It was the most logical path the killer would've taken. There were no caves in this area. Only sheer cliffs, decreasing blue sky and unending miles of trees and dirt. The canyon that led north was where Lila had predicted the killer would go, and so would Branch.

His socked foot slipped off the boulder beneath him, and his entire body shifted out of alignment. Slapping his hands out to stop himself from face-planting into the next rock, he breathed through the pain streaking up his ankle and into his calf. He dragged his foot from between the boulders. Still in one piece, but there was no telling how long that would last.

He growled to provide his frustration an outlet. In vain. There was no outlet. Not as long as Lila was out here, potentially in danger from the same killer who'd stabbed Sarah Lantos. That core tension would keep winding tighter and tighter until it suffocated him. It would only be released by getting eyes on her. Having her in his arms. Ensuring she'd live another day to threaten ending his.

Branch couldn't help but scan the area for the dozenth time. Sooner or later, Risner and the rest of the rangers would realize something had happened and send aid, but until then, he was all she had. And he wouldn't fail her. He wouldn't abandon her as had so easily been done to him. All he could do was rely on his training to get to her.

Reaching the bottom of boulder mountain, he took another pull of water, but it did nothing for the light-headedness taking advantage. The world threatened to tip out from under him as he took the next step. Then another.

Hell. Maybe he'd hit his head harder than he assumed. The laceration hadn't been deep as far as he could tell, but that didn't mean there wasn't internal bleeding or that he hadn't sustained a concussion.

Didn't matter. He'd push through. He'd been the one to drag Lila into this mess. He'd be the one to get her out of it. Risner had wanted her off the investigation—for no other reason than the man was a sexist son of a bitch—and Branch was hating himself for pulling her back in. She'd had a way out. She'd been safe in her own little bubble, and he should've left her the hell alone.

But he'd been selfish. Wanting her insight, wanting that addictive perfume of hers in his system, wanting her to cheer for him for something as small as finding the killer's campsite. Wanting…her. All of her. The fake persona she wore in front of him and the other rangers, and the woman she'd been trying to hide as long as he'd known her.

And if anything happened to her, he'd live with the consequences of that failure for the rest of his life. Never letting himself rest. Never granting himself forgiveness. So he pushed himself harder, until his vision blurred and Branch didn't know which way was up.

His boot connected with something metallic, and he launched forward to catch himself against a rotting pine tree. Bark came off in his hands as he blinked to get his bearings. Stinging pain blistered along his fingers and in his palms, and he watched as blood blossomed in the cracks. "Damn it."

A metallic cylinder rolled to a stop at the base of the tree. A water bottle. Crouching, Branch took in the dents and scratches interrupting the dark green exterior coating, then allowed himself to take in the rest of his surroundings. The tree provided shade as the temperature climbed but wouldn't do much else as the sky darkened with heavy clouds. A sleeping bag lay crumpled to his left with a supply pack resting at the far end of a makeshift campsite. And a first aid kit—complete with bloodied gauze—had been discarded a few feet away.

"Lila." He tossed the water bottle onto the sleeping bag and headed for the kit. Every pad of gauze had been used. He avoided touching the blood directly, but from the amount that had soaked clean through each pad, he guessed the injury had been severe. Had Lila been injured during the landslide? Had the killer done something to her? Had her abductor tried to stop the bleeding? No responsible hiker would have left their supplies behind. Which meant something had happened.

Tearing into the main compartment of the pack, Brach ripped through the supplies for anything that might give him an idea of who'd killed Sarah Lantos and taken his partner, but couldn't find any ID. A change of clothes, protein bars, electrolyte powder, sunscreen, matches.

And a loaded magazine to a handgun. As well as a handful of blasting caps.

The metal tubes were meant to be inserted into the end of a stick of dynamite with a fuse tied to the end for safe detonation. If there was such a thing. Dynamite itself was notoriously unstable. Any small movement could set it off. The killer wouldn't have carried it around in his pack, which meant the son of a bitch must've stashed it somewhere else.

An echo of an explosion replayed in his head. Right before the landslide.

Branch dug deeper into the pack, almost frantic to prove his theory. Thin twine had been stored closer to the bottom. A fuse. Hell. The killer had triggered the landslide. But to kill him and Lila, or simply to slow them down? Working with dynamite could backfire at any moment. Literally. And now Lila was in the hands of a man who'd weaponized it against them.

Extra gun ammunition had been stuffed in the bottom of the pack. Federal law prohibited hikers from bringing firearms into national parks, but this wasn't the first time Branch had come to terms with the fact that killers didn't like following the rules. No sign of the weapon itself, which meant whoever'd taken Lila had most likely done so at gunpoint. But for what? To help him escape? To hold her as leverage when Branch and the rest of NPS caught up?

Branch shoved to stand, eyes on what he could see of the valley. He watched for any sign of movement but noted nothing but grassland and juniper trees. She was out there. He could feel it.

Lila might indulge in self-deprecating jokes and laugh off verbal attacks from her fellow rangers, but she was a fighter and influential as hell. At the end of this, he wouldn't be surprised if the killer turned himself in with an expression of regret after she was through with him. Until then, Branch would have to take matters into his own hands.

Narrowing his gaze on the canyon that would lead the killer north, he crossed the perimeter of the campsite. "Where are you, Barbie?"

A glimpse of color pulled his attention to a blossoming prickly pear cactus. The yellow flowers looked almost translucent as the sun crested into the second half of the sky. And caught in its needles, a hot pink floral kerchief.

Lila's kerchief.

Oxygen lodged in his chest. She'd been here. He wasn't sure how long ago, but now he had proof. She'd survive the landslide. Only to be taken hostage by a man who'd already killed a woman within the past twenty-four hours.

Branch practically lunged for the fabric, pulling it free. It was softer than he expected, catching on the cuts and calluses on his fingers. The design fit Lila perfectly with black zebra stripes and a border of fringe. He'd barely managed not to roll his eyes at the sight of it this morning at the grotto, but now he could do nothing but hold onto it as though it would provide him insight into her whereabouts.

Hints of her perfume clung to the fabric, and he couldn't help but inhale her sweet tart scent to replace the acrid bitterness collecting at the back of his throat. The effect shot a renewed charge of energy into his veins. Just as the mere sight of Lila had all these months. The kerchief itself had come unknotted, and Branch scanned the distance between where he'd recovered it and the campsite. At least fifteen feet away. She'd left it here. For him. To tell him how to find her. "Clever girl."

His vision threatened to black out as he navigated beyond the patch of prickly pear cacti and down the incline into the deepest part of the valley, gripping her kerchief with everything he had. To keep him conscious. To remind him of what was at stake.

Branch had spent his entire life judging others for their lack of discipline, for failing to follow through, keep their word and hold people accountable for their actions, good and bad. Every standard he'd set for himself, he expected of others, but walking in on his wife and his best friend in bed together had taught him that devotion didn't mean the same to them as it meant to him.

But all that had gone to hell once Lila Jordan had surgically inserted herself into his life with enthusiastic smiles, ridiculous death threats and frenzied schemes to encourage people to get to know her. She was nothing if not devoted. He saw it in the way she held onto her secrets, how she clung to a personality she'd created, when she went out of her way to make everyone else comfortable at the expense of her own peace.

Where Branch had stood his ground—hoping others accepted him for who he was, but not upset or disappointed when they didn't—Lila moved mountains and parted seas. He'd fought that charismatic influence as long as he could, and it hadn't done him a damn bit of good. She'd gotten to him, and there was nothing he could do to convince himself she hadn't earned a place in his life. Whatever that looked like from here on out, he didn't care. He only wanted her safe.

Forcing one foot in front of the other, Branch picked up the pace as the downhill dragged him deeper into Zion's backcountry. Ponderosa pines jutted up from the earth and cut off his view of the rest of the valley, closing in on him, but allowed enough room for him to pass.

The trees here had burned black, stripped of their foliage and growth for the foreseeable future due to a lightning strike that'd sparked a forest fire two years ago, turning the area into a barren wasteland. He couldn't help but compare these trees with the black remnants of his insides, charred, weak, serving no other purpose than to decompose over time for the greater good. He couldn't deny his desire to steal Lila's light for himself—to give him something to hope for—but there wasn't anything he could gift her in return. He was like these trees. Dead inside, waiting for the last straw to break him completely.

Branch slowed at the smallest glimpse of green at the base of one of the burned trees. There, fighting from the depths of the blackened wood against all odds, a pink-petaled flower had begun blooming. As if in challenge. To prove that even dead things still had the potential to create something beautiful.

Then a scream tore through the valley.

Chapter Fifteen

Pain arched straight down her front.

Rock cut into Lila's chest, palms and hips as the weight on her back held her in place. Agony ripped through her scalp as the killer pulled her hair back, forcing her upper body off the ground. Another scream tore from her throat, echoing down the canyon a mere few hundred feet in front of her.

She'd almost made it. She'd almost escaped.

But despite the wound in the killer's leg, he'd somehow caught up to her. Had tackled her from behind. Driving a knee into her spine, he pressed his mouth against her ear. "Hello, darling."

Tears burned in her eyes, but she wouldn't let them fall. Not for this asshole. Her lungs had yet to get the message to start functioning again. They spasmed from the impact as she clawed at his hand in her hair.

In a move any professional wrestler would be proud of, the killer flipped her onto her back with ease. His knees locked down on her arms, holding her in place. "What did I tell you would happen if you ran, Ranger Jordan?"

The sun glared down on her, blocking his features, but she didn't need for him to see her clearly for him to kill her. Or to feel the gun pressed against her temple. The metal was surprisingly cold in a landscape toasting at a pleasant one hundred and six degrees.

"It's amateurs like you who give kidnapping a bad name. I mean, come on. Didn't you see the water bottle coming?"

The words were a farce. A desperate attempt to distract her brain from recognizing these were her final moments. Her laugh—something along the lines of hysteric and disassociated—cut between them. "You should've seen your face."

He dragged the barrel from her head down her cheek, clutching her jaw with his free hand. His strength was enough to leave bruises if she walked away from this alive. "That mouth of yours just doesn't stop, does it?"

"I've met scarecrows with more spine than you." The words were garbled due to the restraint on her jaw, but based on the contortion of his expression, she felt he got the gist. Pushing against his knees, Lila fought to free her arms, but he only shifted his weight forward. She bucked her hips. Again, going nowhere. She pinched her eyes shut against the frustrated growl trying to escape. Oh, dang. No wonder Branch growled at her so often. This was aggravating as hell. "Get off me."

"You're exhausting, you know that? No wonder someone tried to cut your throat." He set the barrel of the gun beneath her chin, then dragged it across the scar tissue spanning from the right side of her neck to the left. "They wanted to steal your voice, didn't they? Wanted to shut you up. Maybe I should be the one to finish a job. Hmm?"

His words hurt more than she wanted to admit, and the first tear fell. Shame spiked through her, and she tried to buck him free again, but it was no use. He held her steady, pinned against the very earth she'd worked so hard to protect from people like him. People who didn't appreciate the beautiful things in life. Who saw something fragile and pushed it to the breaking point. Who walked through this world with the expectation for everyone else to fall on their knees in gratitude for their mere presence. People like her brother-in-law.

"No, no, no. Don't cry, Ranger Jordan." Lowering his face over hers, he cocked his head to one side, studying her as the park geologists studied sediment rates under a microscope. His breath fanned down her neck, over her scar, until it was all she could focus on. "Relax. I'll make it quick. You won't even feel a thing."

Don't scream, Lila. Every time you fight me, I'll make it hurt more.

That voice. It didn't belong to the killer. The words played on repeat until the man in front of her didn't exist at all.

She was back in her bedroom in her parents' basement. His hand clamped over her mouth, pressing her deeper into her pillow. It hurt. The way he handled her. She didn't know how it was possible she hadn't heard him come into her room. She'd locked the door, hadn't she? She locked it every night since he'd moved in upstairs, noting the way he watched her do the dishes or how his face changed when she came home sweaty from soccer practice. She couldn't see his face right now, but she knew every angle from their time together over the years. Every line. Even the jagged scar down the side of his face. From a fight, he'd told her, but something about him being in her room in the middle of the night—pressing her into the mattress with his weight and nothing but whispers—made her think tonight wasn't the first time he'd done this. That maybe he hadn't escaped unscathed. He pried his hand from her face, trusting her not to scream. But she'd never taken well to following orders.

Lila screamed into her attacker's face, and he reared back.

It was all the chance she needed as his knees briefly lifted off her arms. She dug her fingernails into his face and scratched downward as hard as she could, her survival instincts consuming logic.

His scream fed into a sick satisfaction a split second before the gun slammed against her head. Lightning exploded behind her eyes as she fell back, but the need to escape had already taken hold. She shoved her bloodied palms into his chest as hard as she could. He fell back, pinned her legs to the ground, but it was enough. The gun went with him. Snapping out of his grip, it landed too far away for her to grab.

Lila flipped onto her stomach. *Run.* All she could do was run. She pushed upright. Her toes failed to leverage packed, cracked dirt, and her boot slipped out from underneath her. She went down but managed to get her balance as the killer fought for his. She pumped her legs as hard as she could. She'd been training for this day. Every single true crime podcast had led her to this moment. With his DNA under her blood-crusted fingernails, she'd give the National Park Service everything she could to identify her killer.

"You bitch!" Pure rage laced those two words. Too close. How the hell did he manage to stay on her heels with that wound?

Aiming for the canyon mouth, Lila maneuvered over a felled tree that hadn't survived the forest fire two years ago. Her hot pink boot lace caught on a branch, and she thrust her leg forward to break through. The overly loud snap gave up her position, but she wouldn't stop. Couldn't. A cool breeze taunted her from the canyon entrance. She was going to make it. She didn't have any other choice as the memories of that night in her bedroom waited for the smallest sliver of her attention.

She hated this feeling. Helplessness. Weakness. Pain. It was too similar to those horrifying minutes a man she was told to trust had turned into a monster. Her throat convulsed as though she was right back there in that basement, a scream trapped in her throat.

Shadows crept toward her as the cliffs took shape on either side. Her skin cooled instantly as she scrambled along the riverbed. Smooth stones and awkwardly angled trees growing out of the rock face threatened to trip her up. The canyon itself offered little protection from the killer at her back, but without the sun beating down on her, she felt more herself. Clearheaded.

She couldn't go like this for miles. She'd already burned through the hit of caffeine from this morning and hadn't eaten more than a protein bar before the landslide. Every step took her deeper into Zion wilderness, where the rangers assigned to the backcountry patrolled few and far between. She was actively running away from help, and the killer must know that. He was isolating her. Keeping her from seeking help. Prey to his predator.

Hide. She needed a place to hide, then she could worry about contacting NPS and making sure search and rescue looked for Branch.

Lila shut down the sob fighting for release. No. She couldn't think like that. He was alive. They were going to make it out of this and meet up for coffee the next time neither of them had a shift to cover. He'd given her his word. It was all she could focus on as a dark hole took shape in the rock face up ahead.

A cave.

It sat about twenty feet off the canyon floor with a few rocks and trees acting as stairs if she was careful. It was also the first place the killer would look for her. And potentially where she could be eaten alive by the mountain cougars that lived in the park. But she had to take the risk.

Her palms screamed in protest as she hauled herself up the first oddly angled tree. The bark fell away under her weight, and she slammed into the wall at her side. Rock grated against her exposed skin, but she pushed to the next obstacle. This would make a great audition for *American Gladiator*.

Darkness enveloped her as she reached the mouth of the cave. Cold air raised the hair on the back of her neck. It was damp and smelled of carnage and decomposition. Something definitely lived in this cave full-time, and she hoped whatever it was had gone hunting instead of waiting for food to walk right in the front door.

The cave curved deeper into the mountain, cutting off the only source of light at the mouth, but distance didn't ease the tension knotting in her stomach. Wetness clung to the walls and soaked into her uniform, and it took everything in her not to groan out of disgust. It'd take a miracle to get the decomposition smell out of cotton. She could already see Risner's signature drying on another write-up for disgracing her uniform.

Cringing against the sticky substance now coating her hands, she moved deeper into the cave.

"I know you're in here, Ranger Jordan. You can't hide from me."

Movement echoed down the tunnel of the cave, accentuating every word out of the killer's mouth. She hadn't heard him follow her inside. How had he managed to keep his footsteps from bouncing off the rock walls? Or had she not noticed due to the chaos in her head?

"I know every inch of this park." He was getting closer. "Most likely better than you."

Fresh images reserved for her nightmares were right there on the cusp of her waking mind, but she couldn't think about that right now. Lila felt her way deeper into the cave. This was a bad idea, but it was the only option she had right now. She'd brained him with his own water bottle, then scratched caverns down his face. Nope. She wasn't getting out of this alive if he had anything to say about it. "Why did you kill Sarah Lantos?"

His low laugh leaked into her body like a cold drip that stole her body temperature. "Some people deserve to die. Sarah was one of them. She made me suffer by keeping her secret all these years. Threatened everyone I cared about. I granted her a mere taste of my pain by stabbing her. But then she had to go trip on a rock and fall over the edge of the cliff. Ended my fun too soon."

Lila's gut clenched. "Do I deserve to suffer?"

She hadn't meant to ask the question. Didn't want to give him any sort of power over her, but there it was. The one question she'd asked herself a thousand times since the fallout of her actions from that night. Did she deserve to suffer? Her family certainly thought so. Sometimes she did, too. Maybe this was always going to be her ending.

But then why had the universe allowed Branch to come into her life?

"You're just like her, you know." Gravel grated nearby, and then she could feel him. Right in front of her. As though he'd simply thought of her location and appeared.

His outline solidified the longer she begged her vision to catch up. As did the gun. "You latch onto your targets by pretending to be something you're not, then manipulate them into following your agenda. And for that, you're going to die."

A gunshot exploded.

Chapter Sixteen

He heard the shot.

It punctured the canyon, reverberating through him as though he'd been hit with the sound barrier. Branch slowed to pinpoint the source.

There was no denying that gut-wrenching explosion. He'd heard it multiple times over his years as a ranger in the parks. Thudding and terrifying. And everything in him froze at the realization. Blood drained from his upper body in a rush that nearly knocked him on his ass. "Lila!"

He hadn't been fast enough. He'd followed that single scream across the valley with everything he had left, and it still hadn't been enough. The pain in his head intensified as Branch navigated the uneven terrain of the dry riverbed. He wouldn't be too late. He couldn't be too late. Because that meant he'd failed her and wasted four solid months trying to keep his distance from her when he should have run at her full speed.

Lila had brought a spark into his life. Gifted him glimpses of color in an otherwise black-and-white world. She'd made him feel when he wanted nothing more than to sink into the numbness left behind by his ex-wife and best friend's betrayal. She gave him purpose. A reason to keep going. This wasn't how it was supposed to end.

Two days of standing at her side wasn't enough, damn it. "Where are you?"

The canyon swallowed him whole, rising on either side of him as if leading him into a trap. Walls of red, black and white rock towered above him but gave no indication of where the shot had come from. Cool air rippled goose bumps across his bare arms. Hell, his head hurt. He could feel warm liquid tracking down his face. The butterfly bandage had soaked through with blood, warning him not to push it, but Lila needed him. His heart threatened to beat straight out of his chest with every step. "Come on. Come on."

Dragging his hand through his hair, he did the hardest thing he'd ever had to do during his time as a ranger. Wait. For something—anything—that might tell him where she'd been taken.

A low growl reached his ears. The canyon wall moved.

Wait, that wasn't right.

Fur, the same color as the rock, shifted to his right, revealing the powerful body of a mountain lion. And, damn, it was big. Most likely male. Mountain lions didn't normally go looking for trouble, but when you just happened to walk into their territory, you were fair game.

Every muscle down Branch's spine hardened with battle-ready tension. Hell, all he could think about was how Lila would smile and want to pet the beast, and that thought alone helped calm his racing heart. She'd probably want to adopt it and bring it back home. Call it something like Fluffy or Pumpkin just to get a rise out of him. "You don't look like a Pumpkin, which means she'll probably call you Fluffy."

The oversize cat hissed, exposing sharp, elongated teeth meant to snap one of his arms in half. Branch backed up a few steps as the cat descended from its perch, cutting off his access to the rest of the canyon. To Lila.

Raising his arms out in front of him as though Fluffy could acknowledge his surrender—was he really calling this thing Fluffy?—he brought his pack around to his front. Slowly unzipping the top of his pack, he dragged the unopened bag of beef jerky—teriyaki flavored, of course—into the open and popped the seal. "You like jerky?"

Mountain lions averaged two to three feet in height, but this one had obviously been eating his spinach. Impressive muscle rippled along the cat's back as it gauged the threat Branch presented. Another growl penetrated the space between them in warning. The animal had to have a den nearby. Potentially behind it. Where Lila could be.

Rangers were trained to deal with wild animals, mostly to avoid them and warn hikers to do the same, but Branch maintained eye contact as he tossed a chunk of jerky behind him a good twenty feet. "Go get it."

Did mountain lions take commands? He wasn't sure. But just as Dr. Grant baited the T. rex, Branch tossed a second helping of jerky and froze. Unwilling to do anything more to provoke the animal. He was going to die. It was as simple as that, but he'd go down fighting if necessary.

The cat stared at him with those black eyes surrounded by yellow, looking for all the world as if he wanted to roll his eyes. Then he gave up the staring contest and ambled straight past Branch and closer to the jerky. Seemed Fluffy really did like jerky. Branch would have to remember that. Then again, one mountain lion sighting was enough to last him a lifetime.

Now a whole new fear had taken root again. Not being able to get to Lila.

Branch took a furtive step deeper into the canyon, not stupid enough to take his eyes off Fluffy as the cat gobbled up the jerky. The cat wrenched its head back and forth trying to chomp down on the meat. Okay, so Branch had broken the cardinal rule of not feeding the wildlife, but it was for a good reason. And if he had to come back here every day with a bag of jerky to make up for it, he would. As long as Lila made it out of this canyon in one piece.

A cave took shape ahead. The perfect den for a mountain lion willing to kill anything that came near it. Fluffy was preoccupied with his free meal. This was the only shot Branch would have. "Lila!"

No answer.

His voice echoed off the canyon walls, and he'd never felt so utterly alone in his life. As though his separation from Lila had torn something important from his very being.

How was that possible? How in a matter of two days had she become more vital than his next breath? He couldn't take it anymore, this emptiness. He'd thrived in isolation, telling himself he was better off alone, that he didn't need anyone, not wanting to infect others with his pain, but Ranger Barbie had patched a few of the holes eaten away by his divorce. And he wanted more. He wanted her back.

Scrambling up the odd footholds leading to the mouth of the cavern, Branch slapped his hand against the rock wall for something to hold onto. His head had other plans. It thudded hard with every breath. Darkness wrapped around him in a sickening blanket, but he pushed on. The reward far outweighed the risks.

Slickness coated his hands as he followed the natural curve of the cave, leaving Fluffy and the safety of the park behind. He hauled his pack forward and extracted his flashlight. Hitting the power button, Branch studied the walls—too close together—and patches of tan fur littering the cave floor. Uneven rock threatened to trip him up as he searched for any sign Lila had sought the cave in a last-ditch attempt—

A wall of muscle slammed into him from the left.

His back hit the wall, crushing the air from his lungs. A metallic barrel pressed into his head, but Branch shot his hand upward.

A gunshot exploded next to his ear, triggering a high-pitched ringing that drowned his groan. The second shot rained rock and dust onto his head, and instinct had him knocking the weapon clean from his attacker's hand. The gun skittered across the cave floor, out of sight.

A forearm locked across throat. Branch tried to breathe around the weight, but the killer had the upper hand. Based on the angled beam of his discarded flashlight, the man at his throat clocked in a few inches taller than Branch, but he didn't have the muscle.

Pressure built in his chest as his lungs worked to supply oxygen to his starving limbs. Spit and sweat combined on his face. Inky black tendrils webbed his vision. He was going to pass out any second. Branch wedged his knee up, colliding with the killer's gut. Once. Twice. Still, the bastard's hold refused to release.

Throwing everything he had left into his right hook, Branch connected with the killer's temple. A responding groan accompanied the smallest of releases across his throat, and Branch sucked in a breath. But then he was weightless, the cave floor rushing to meet him. He rolled into the opposite wall, barely catching sight of the outline descending on him.

"Branch!" Lila's voice filled the cavern. Filled him. She was alive. Rushing toward her abductor with one arm raised, she brought down what looked like a rock in her palm, but the killer managed to avoid it colliding with his head. The makeshift weapon bounced off the man's back.

Branch fought to catch his breath. He dug his fingers into the rock floor when his head wanted to do nothing but surrender. "Lila, run."

The killer turned on her. Faster than Lila could counter, the back of his hand slammed against her cheek. Lila hit the ground hard. She lay there, unmoving.

"Lila!" Branch shot to his feet. every cell in his body on fire. The rage he kept at a simmer unleashed as he tackled the son of bitch to the ground. Fisting both hands in the killer's shirt, he dragged his attacker forward, then rammed his head against the rock floor.

A scraping sound reached his ears. The gun. Catching sight of the weapon's outline, Branch scrambled to get his hands on it. He dove. Realizing his mistake too late.

The killer planted a hand at the back of Branch's skull and shoved his face straight into the nearest wall. Cold metal pressed into Branch's cheek as he worked to regain his bearings, sobering him instantly.

"You're wrong if you think she's worth saving, Ranger Thompson. She's nothing but a liar. A manipulator who will choose her own survival over you. She doesn't care about you. She never will."

His insides coiled as Branch locked his gaze on Lila's unconscious form. That rage bubbled over again, out of control as he set both hands against the wall and pushed back, knocking the killer off-balance. He swept his hand out, latching onto his assailant's wrist and twisted until bone and tendon snapped. The knife fell into his free hand, and Branch pressed the tip to the killer's throat. "You don't know anything about her."

"Do you?" A sickening low laugh filled the cave. "Or do you just think you do?" And he rocketed a fist into Branch's face.

Branch went down, the knife still clutched in his hand. But when he turned in expectation of the next threat, the outline of his attacker was gone. Branch dove for the flashlight, spearing the beam over every inch of the cave. Damn it all to hell.

The killer had gotten away.

Adrenaline drained from his body in a rush as movement shifted to his left. "Lila."

"Branch?" A sob cut off her sweet voice.

Dropping the flashlight, he pulled her lightweight frame into his chest. "It's okay. I've got you. I'm here. I'm here."

The tears turned to full-blown sobs as she wrapped her arms around his neck and held on for dear life. Her perfume—muted through the metallic scent of blood and sweat—settled his high-strung nervous system.

He soothed his hand down the back of her head, noting she'd lost her Stetson. "I've got you. You're safe now, and I'm never letting you go."

Chapter Seventeen

Her body had stopped obeying her commands a couple hours ago. Lila rolled over on the sleeping bag, the material sticking to every inch of her back. The tent Branch had set up once they'd left the canyon wore its age well. The bright orange dye had faded from use in the sun, but the mesh windows, canvas and zippers all did their jobs.

She wasn't sure how long she'd been asleep. Couldn't really remember anything past the cave. Of being in Branch's arms. He must've brought her here, but after a cursory search, she realized she'd woken alone.

Her skin felt too tight and sticky. What she wouldn't give for her crappy, stained shower in her crappy little rented house with her crappy twin bed. Never again would she take it for granted.

A low rumble of a voice drew her attention to the zippered tent flap. She couldn't make out the words, but the cadence and tenor soothed all the aches and stings after a few seconds. Branch. The tent itself didn't fit much more than two sleeping bags with some space at the foot for her pack.

Wait. How did…

A headache speared through her brain at the thought of all the events that'd led to the cave: the landslide, barely escaping being pulverized by those boulders, leaving her pack for Branch to find…

He'd come for her. He hadn't given up.

Dragging herself from the now-soaked sleeping bag, Lila reached for the zipper and maneuvered it around the curve of the door. Blistering pain seeped down her arm from where the killer's first bullet had grazed her. She'd been lucky. One inch to the left, and she might not have made it out of that cave alive. "Oh, hell. That hurts."

Footsteps ricocheted through her head a split second before the rest of the tent flap was ripped back, revealing the dark-eyed mountain of a man on the other side. "You should be resting."

She didn't have the energy to keep her arm up, even with the fresh bandage secured around the wound. Had Branch patched her up? Well, that was a stupid question. Sarah Lantos's killer certainly hadn't done it. Despite the fact the sun had begun its descent behind the surrounding cliffs, bruising the sky to a deep purple, she blinked against the sensory onslaught, squinting one eye as she looked up at him. "How long was I out?"

"A few hours." His expression refused to give her anything of substance. He'd locked himself up nice and tight. "How do you feel?"

"You remember that skunk that got hit by a car at the visitor's center, and none of the rangers wanted to go near it because the stink sack had exploded?" Using the tent frame, she pulled herself to her feet. Her head swam. Mistake. She'd made a mistake. "Like that."

She practically stumbled into the campsite he'd built while she'd been unconscious. Rangers didn't believe in campfires, so while the killer had arranged a ring of stones to contain the flames and stay warm back at his site, Branch had set up an electric lantern in the center of theirs. He'd emptied his pack, lining his food and supplies out in the open. "You've been busy."

Looking at him—really looking at him—she noted the dried blood at the side of his face, the dark circles beneath his eyes. White crystals clung to the underside of his chin. It happened when the body sweated too much salt. Bruising took shape around his jaw. He was standing, but barely. And had apparently lost a shoe somewhere along the way. "Figured it'll take a day for us to get back to headquarters. I needed to see what we had left in supplies."

"And?" She cataloged what he'd gathered. It wasn't enough between them.

"You should eat something." His shoulders bunched as though expecting an argument, but her stomach was basically eating itself as they stood here and talked about food.

Accepting a protein bar and a banana, she nearly collapsed at the edge of the campsite. Her fingers ached as she peeled the banana skin away, and while she'd never been a fan of the overly sweet—sometimes mushy—fruit, it was possibly the best thing she'd ever eaten in her life.

The pressure of being watched raised the hairs on the back of her neck, and she looked up to see Branch studying her. As though ensuring she got everything she needed before he dared take care of himself. "Have you slept?" she asked.

"No." He moved around the campsite, taking up position opposite. As far from her as he could get.

Well, that hurt. Hadn't they just survived a killer together? Hadn't they moved past one-word answers and growls? Or did she really smell that bad? Lila made an attempt to casually check her underarms and cringed at the bitter odor clinging to her uniform…and other parts of her body. But he couldn't be any better.

She shuddered at the physical distance he'd set between them, still feeling his arms around her as he'd carried her out of that cave. He'd saved her. Fought a killer for her. And now… Lila focused on one bite after another. She'd survived the landslide, a kidnapping, a gunshot wound and the crushing hopelessness that came with all of it. At some point exhaustion had won out, and right now, she didn't have the energy to chase Branch's affection. "The killer knew Sarah Lantos. Said he was punishing her for making him suffer."

Branch kept his attention on his metal water bottle, the light from the lantern carving deeper shadows along his handsome face. And, damn it, her ovaries had donned war paint and started metaphorically chucking eggs at the man after everything he must've faced to get to her. "What else?"

"What do you mean?" She had to snap herself out of this haze. Being in Branch's thrall was far more dangerous than having been taken hostage by a killer in a lot of ways. Sure, Sarah Lantos's killer could do physical damage, but her partner had so many weapons at his disposal to destroy her in every other way.

"What else did he say to you?"

Her throat dried. Emotion lodged where she was pretty sure she'd killed it off years ago, but she just couldn't tell him the truth. Not without risking him looking at her like every other ranger had over the years. And she couldn't go back to that. Not with him. Not after everything they'd survived together. "I don't remember a whole lot, but the little I do, it seems our victim isn't who we thought she was. This is also coming from the man who stabbed her, so take that with a grain of salt."

Branch let that sit between them, and she hated his silence. His distance. It made the grime coating her skin burn and itch, but there was nothing she could do to wash it away. After a few minutes and seeing that she'd finished her dinner, Branch shoved to stand, tossing his water bottle at his feet. "I need to assess your injuries."

It was easy to paste her practiced smile back on and slip into that protective layer she'd created to block out all the bad. Spreading her arms wide, Lila leaned back to get a better view of his face in the last offering of sunset. "Have your way with me, Ranger Thompson. I promise not to bite. Unless you're into that."

"You were nearly killed." A scowl contorted his face, a sucker punch straight to the gut. Ah, there he was. The grizzly bear had returned, and everything they'd been through together suddenly didn't seem so bad.

That was okay. She was used to people running the other direction once they realized she was more than they'd bargained for. She'd just wanted things to be different with him. "In my defense, I was left unsupervised."

His fingers splayed across her skin, right over the ring of gauze on her arm, but he was careful not to prod or poke anywhere that might hurt. The lines between his brows deepened as he unwrapped her like a delicate piece of china. Or the way she unwrapped her first helping of Cherry Garcia. Either way, heat spread under her skin at his touch. "Did you pick up anything that might identify the killer?"

Right. This wasn't personal. He'd made that very clear by keeping his distance unless absolutely necessary. Like making sure she didn't bleed out in the middle of the desert on his shift. "Does his astrological sign count? Because that man is definitely a Sagittarius. Egotistical, impatient, boastful. Pretty sure him and Ted Bundy would've gotten along well together."

He didn't have an answer for that. Pain flared up her arm, and she tried to drag herself out of his touch, but Branch held on tight.

"He didn't really introduce himself, but in my head, I called him Covid." Lila tried to even her breathing, but it was so much harder when a six-plus mountain of eye candy insisted on groping her.

Branch's mouth twitched at one corner. So…he wasn't entirely as unaffected as he was trying to be, which only pissed her off more. The break in his composure didn't last long as he raised his gaze to her throat. To the ugly, thick scar she couldn't bear to look at in the mirror. He brought his hand up, his thumb brushing the underside of her neck. "The kerchiefs."

It took her a second to realize he was talking about her attempt to hide her shame from him and the rest of the world.

"Who hurt you?" Those three words again. That was all it took to shake the dragging haze of exhaustion free.

Her skin boiled under his touch, and Lila couldn't take much more. She pulled free of his hand, not bothering to rewrap her wound. Probably a stupid choice, but her choice all the same. Her poor heart slammed against her ribs at the concern in his voice. The anger on her behalf. Compared to the bruises on her ribs and the massive headache telling her she hadn't had enough to drink while running for her life, she'd take another bullet graze than face this conversation. She headed back for the tent, not really sure where else to go. It wasn't as though she could just run for the hills. Those hills had a killer in them. One who'd already gotten too close. "No one."

"Lila." Her name on his lips pulled her up short. Had he ever called her that?

As much as she hated the idea of him joining in the other rangers' Barbie games, she wasn't sure her heart could handle him seeing past the persona she'd designed. Through the smiles and the makeup and the pink kerchiefs. There was a reason she felt safer as Ranger Barbie. Most people—Risner, Sayles and all the other rangers, hikers even—made their assumptions and avoided taking the time to look deeper. Like the glitter she'd applied on her cheeks would infect them. Herpes of the craft world, for the win.

But Branch said her name as though he intended to do just that. Become infected. Dig deeper. And she was scared of what he might find. Would he still want to meet her for coffee after this investigation was over? Would he be able to look her in the eye when he learned the truth? How truly broken she really was.

"Barbies don't feel pain, remember?" If only that were true. The memories that had held her captive more so than the man with the gun threatened to resurface.

A hand clasped over her mouth. Threats in her ear. The weight of her attacker in a room where she should've been safe. It wasn't that night that gave her nightmares or had led her to pasting on the smiles Branch seemed to see right through. It was everything that happened afterward, and at the lowest point in her life, stripped of everything and everyone she'd ever loved, she'd stretched out a hand to find something to hold onto. In a mess of blood and hopelessness in the very room where she'd been made a victim over and over again, her fingers had folded around a Barbie doll from her childhood. And she'd felt… happy. For the first time in years, she had something good in her hands.

It only made sense to carry that feeling with her to fight back the demons closing in. "Nobody hurt me, Branch. I did it to myself."

Chapter Eighteen

In this new concept called caring, Branch was finding quite a few things to hate. Mostly the changes in himself.

He'd waited outside the tent while Lila had changed into a new set of clothes, presumably wanting to be free of blood and grime after she'd helped irrigate the wound at his temple. He'd waited as her movements slowed. Waited as the night grew cold and her breathing grew even. He hadn't been able to face her.

Nobody hurt me, Branch. I did it to myself.

The jagged scar across her neck was unlike anything he'd ever seen. At least not on a person still walking the earth. The moment he'd dragged her from that damn cave and into the open, it'd stared back at him. Crystallizing a deep need to destroy anyone and anything that'd had a hand in marring her perfect skin. He hadn't trusted himself to get near her, afraid all that rage would burn her if he got too close. So he'd set himself up on the opposite side of camp, to protect her, but he'd only managed to feed the hollowness in his chest to the point he couldn't breathe.

Except there was no one to fight.

She'd done it to herself. Why? What could've possibly happened to convince her the only choice she had was death?

Branch pocketed the protein bar wrapper, not really tasting the ingredients. His senses had dulled in the time he'd been separated from Lila and had gone mute since she'd zipped herself inside the tent. Damn it. What he wouldn't give to go back to pretending she didn't exist. To shutting himself away from the rest of the world and avoiding this new rip in his heart that focused entirely on Lila's well-being.

His skin prickled as temperatures dropped. Branch kept his attention on the mouth of the canyon, waiting for the next threat to make another move. The killer had escaped the cave. A quick search for the gun turned up empty.

And it was only a matter of time before his body failed him. He'd driven it to the edge too many times today. Surviving the landslide, searching for Lila, luring a mountain lion with jerky and then fighting off a killer. Worse, at some point, he'd come to accept he wouldn't witness Lila's smile ever again. That he'd lost her. The pinch in his chest had yet to get the message she was alive and breathing on the other side of the stretch of canvas between them. Some part of him was still back in that cave, seeing her unconscious. Unmoving.

Something had split open in him then. Pieces of the man he used to be had surfaced with all the rage, and hell, it scared him the lengths he would've gone to get one more second, one more death threat, with her.

Or do you only think you know her? The killer's parting words had seared into his brain and refused to give him respite. They'd surged with every hyperaware glance in her direction, every move she'd made tonight, every word out of her mouth.

Lila was keeping secrets. She wasn't the person she

projected to the world, and while Branch recognized everyone had parts of themselves they didn't want exposed, he thought he'd given her more than enough reason to trust him in the past two days. Everything they'd been through, everything they'd survived—it meant something. Didn't it?

His ex had kept secrets. Had been sleeping with his best friend from work for months before Branch had caught them. She hadn't told him about the pregnancy, about her decision to end it until he'd discovered the truth. Hadn't given him a choice in the matter, and an acidic taste clung to the back of his throat at the idea Lila might do the same. She could hurt him. Whether she knew it or not, Lila had more power over him than he'd allowed anyone to hold since his divorce.

Scrubbing a hand down his face, Branch stopped the thoughts in their tracks. There wasn't a single similarity between Lila and his ex-wife. Exhaustion had won out. The killer had merely tried to get into his head, and hell, the son of a bitch had done a fantastic job. He stood, collecting the electric lantern on his way, and slowly unzipped the tent door.

The sound of Lila's even breathing reached him as he stepped inside. Soft and feminine and bordering a little on snoring. It was cute. He set the lantern at the opposite end of the tent to keep from waking her. After everything they'd been through today, she deserved the rest. But tomorrow they'd have to return to headquarters. They'd have to admit they lost track of the killer, that they didn't have any identifying markers other than his appearance—and maybe his astrology sign. Branch wasn't really looking forward to that conversation with Risner, but he'd sure as hell take it over the silent treatment Lila had given him since retreating to the tent.

He undressed, leaving himself in his undershirt and briefs, before crawling over to his sleeping bag. The tent allowed two people to sleep side by side, but there wasn't a whole lot of room for him to keep his distance. He could still catch hints of Lila's perfume, feel her body heat as he settled on his back.

A soft moan filled the tent, and he froze. Waiting. Every nerve ending he owned had tuned to her movements, those little sighs she made in her sleep. It was enough to stir his insides with something he hadn't allowed himself to feel for a long time. After a few minutes of strained silence and a whole lot of inappropriate thoughts on how to get her to make that noise again, Branch rolled onto his side, away from her, and closed his eyes.

A coldness that had nothing to do with the temperature set in, his skin tightening to the point of pain around his bones. His head pounded. Even after the way he'd treated her—as nothing more than an inconvenience—Lila had insisted on taking care of his wound and watched him force down a couple of ibuprofen from his first aid kit. Though she'd given talking a break.

That was how he'd known how deeply he'd hurt her by pulling away, and he hated himself for it. After everything they'd survived, she still felt the need to put his health first. Freaking hell. How did she keep going? The looks and whispers behind her back from Risner and all the other rangers, the obvious trauma she'd suffered at her own hand, whatever had driven her to take that step, her brush with a killer in that cave, Branch's disregard and flat-out rejection. How hadn't life beaten her down as thoroughly as it'd beaten him?

Lila was strong. Stronger than him, that was for damn sure, and he couldn't stop whatever this new connection was between them in its tracks. But he didn't know how to do this anymore. Have...feelings for someone else. The blackened organ in his chest had stopped trying after the divorce, but then Lila had come along with the promise of light, and his entire being had latched onto it and refused to let go. And crossing that line, admitting he needed her...

His ex-wife had taken his trust and utterly destroyed it right in front of him. Years of good memories and laughs and future plans instantly ash. And he hadn't seen it coming. Marriage had always been the plan, ever since they'd met in high school from their too-small hometown in the middle of Montana. They'd graduated together, gone off to college together, gotten married a couple years afterward and planned their entire lives together. Vacations, late nights filled with sex and promises and *I love you*s, sacrifices for each other's careers.

An entire life built with the one person he'd trusted instantly shattered the day he thought he saw his best friend's car driving down his street as Branch left for the office. His gut had told him to turn around, just as it was telling him to trust Lila now. What would've happened had he not followed his intuition that day? What would happen now if he did?

Awareness spread down his spine as he brushed against Lila's knee. Without checking over his shoulder, he felt she'd turned into him. Seeking him out unconsciously, and hell, if that wasn't adding kindling to the fire. He'd spent so long proving he didn't need anyone. He wasn't sure how to let himself rely on another person again.

A growl resonated in his chest as a result of the battle occupying his head.

Lila shifted at his back. Closer? "Do you want to know what Barbie taught me?"

Her sleep-graveled voice dragged him over hot coals, to the point every cell in his body focused solely on the heat building low in his stomach. It was a rush of fire that would take one very specific thing to put out. One specific woman.

"What?" Branch angled his head over his shoulder. He didn't have to see her clearly for his brain to fill in all those sharp features he'd memorized since setting foot in Zion. The shape of her mouth, a little fuller on one side than the other, the arch of her brows, how much of her dark roots had grown in. The only thing he hadn't committed to memory was that scar, though he couldn't banish the sight of it from his mind.

"Barbie. I used to play with them as a kid. I had a whole collection with the Dreamhouse and the cars and the campers, all the accessories. People think Barbie gives little girls poor body image, but those dolls taught me that you can't reattach a head once it's been removed from the body." Her voice vaulted from one extreme—carefree and light—to deadpan. "So be quiet and let me sleep."

He couldn't hold back the chuckle rumbling through his chest. Hell, this woman hit all the right buttons. Testing his patience, challenging everything he thought he knew about her. He'd been wrong to disregard her as nothing more than a shallow, teasing, high-maintenance diva. Lila Jordan might have a free spirit, but she was probably the most sincere, upbeat and imaginative person he'd ever met. She had to be to come up with those death threats on the daily. "Good night, Lila."

"Branch?" The confidence in her voice wavered.

His name leaving those perfect lips threw his insides into chaos. He bit down his inclination to repeat himself. Found himself not wanting her silent treatment anymore. "Yeah?"

"Thank you. For coming to get me." Her touch trailed across his shoulder, light as a feather, barely recognizable as anything significant but triggered a rush of sensation down his spine all the same. "I know it would've been easier to call in search and rescue and wait for them to lead the search, but I think they would've been too late. He wanted me dead, and you stopped him."

He couldn't avoid looking at her anymore. Rolling onto his other side, Branch faced off with the beauty before him. Her mascara had flaked and run down her cheeks, her lip gloss gone entirely. Even her eyeshadow, once accentuating those compelling blue eyes, had worn off throughout the day. But she was still the most beautiful thing he'd ever set sights on. "You held your own."

She flattened her mouth into a thin line, biting down on the pillowy cushion of her bottom lip. He smoothed his thumb over it to force her to release. A shimmer of tears reflected in the low light of the electric lantern at the other end of their tent. "I couldn't accept you were dead. I was going to go back to look for you, but he wouldn't let me go."

"I'm right here." Branch closed the short distance between them, crushing his mouth to hers.

Chapter Nineteen

Well, that escalated quickly.

Branch's mouth moved over hers in a frantic, almost consuming pace. It was rough and demanding and everything she'd imagined all those nights she couldn't fall asleep.

Matching every ounce of his urgency, Lila threaded her hands into his hair, nearly dragging him onto her sleeping bag. The hard planes of his body weighed on hers. Not to intimidate as she'd felt that night in her childhood bedroom, but to comfort. Security. This was Branch. She was here, with him, in his tent.

His hands framed her face as though he was afraid she would slip through his fingers, but she had no intention of going anywhere. Of being anywhere other than right here. She'd dreamed about it for so long, but nothing compared to the real thing. His woodsy cedar scent teased her senses, the expert strokes of his tongue drove her body temperature higher and higher, and she could taste the slight hint of peppermint toothpaste they'd both eagerly used for some semblance of normality.

The simmering burn she'd fought off all these months roared to a full-blown inferno as Branch shifted a knee between her legs. A moan charged up her throat. She would've been embarrassed if she wasn't delirious with a need to prolong this moment as much as possible.

There was too many layers between them. Her fingernails found purchase at the small of his back, dragging his T-shirt up between his shoulder blades, and he kissed her deeper. Like he'd been starving for this as much as she had. A growl resonated through his chest as his tongue swept over hers, and from there, she was lost in him. No pain in her ribs, no nightmares waiting to ambush her, no hint of a misdirected killer holding a gun to her head.

There was only Branch. He was everything.

Pulling his lips from hers, he peppered openmouthed kisses along her jaw, slowly making his way down her neck, over her scar. She'd gone out of her way to hide it beneath chokers, kerchiefs and scarves throughout the years, but for the first time, she didn't feel the need to shrink back. Or to distract him from the damage she'd done. Lila worked to catch her breath, aware he'd somehow managed to push the top of her sleeping bag out of the way, but it was quickly lost again as calloused hands memorized her hips and thighs in a furiously slow journey.

An unholy gasp rushed up her throat as his thumb trailed along the waistband of her sleep shorts. Her mind raced with guttural pleas for him to touch her where she needed him the most, but then his hands were gone. A protest built on her lips as he stared down at her, and the fire that'd lit her up from the inside died at the expression on his face.

He'd stopped kissing her.

He'd stopped touching her.

"Branch?" She drew herself onto her elbows, trying to get a better read on what had changed.

Drawing back on his haunches, Branch left her aching and cold. They sat frozen for a few seconds before he squeezed his eyes shut. Severing the connection they'd explored in the past few minutes. And when he looked at her again, not a single trace of his desire for her remained. "Go to sleep, Lila. You'll need your energy to get back to headquarters in the morning."

Acid burned her throat as he took up position on his sleeping bag, rolling away from her. Her heart thudded hard against her ribs. Desperate to know what had changed. What she'd done wrong. Rejection fueled the spiraling thoughts into a tornado she couldn't keep up with. She'd been here before. Every time he'd declined her invitation to check out Springdale, every shift he'd negotiated with other rangers to avoid working with her, every unreturned smile or acknowledgment of her presence.

No matter how hard she'd tried to be his friend, she was always the one left a little more depleted and empty. Lila sank back onto her sleeping bag. Tears burned in her eyes, but she hadn't had enough water today, and she'd already cried so much. She didn't have the energy to let them fall. She rolled onto her side, her back to his, and stared at the tent canvas.

But it wasn't enough.

The shame, the vulnerability, the rejection—it all combined to tighten a sickening knot in her stomach, pushing her from her sleeping bag. She couldn't breathe without getting hints of his cedar scent. Couldn't look anywhere in this tent and not see him. She couldn't stay in this enclosed space when he took up so much space.

Sweat cooled on her neck as she tore through the tent flap and out into the open. The first breath should've cleared her head as she broke the perimeter of the campsite, but it only stoked the uncomfortable feelings further.

As if her very being had come to rely on his proximity and couldn't survive without him.

She'd handled rejection before, but there was only so much she could take. Forcing one foot in front of the other, she put as much distance between them as she could while keeping the tent in sight. Predators patrolled this valley, both of the animalistic and humankind, but she couldn't stay at the campsite, either.

She automatically scratched at her neck, desperate for the feel of her kerchief between her fingers as a distraction from the fiery prickling sensation, but she'd lost that in her attempt to escape the killer. Her fingertips only met scar tissue. Grotesque and jagged and uneven. Ugly.

The killer had been right before. When he'd accused her of putting so much effort into her outward appearance to distract from the nastiness on the inside.

"Lila." Branch's voice broke on her name. He'd sneaked up on her. Or maybe she'd been too stuck in her head to think he'd leave the tent to come after her. Didn't matter. He'd said enough. Not in so many words—because Branch Thompson preferred to speak in growls and disdainful looks—but he'd been easy enough to read. He didn't want her. Nobody wanted her. And maybe that was what hurt the most.

"Go back to the tent, Branch." Her throat clogged with tightness as she pressed her fingers into the largest section of scar tissue, her back to him. She couldn't face him without her armor in place, and it wasn't coming as easily as it should. What she wouldn't give for a seventy-two-hour psych hold right now. What a wasted vacation opportunity. "Otherwise, I'm going to assume you want me to hand out your phone number to every kid in the park and tell them it's their direct line to Santa."

Footsteps scuffled over dirt. Getting louder, closer. And then he was standing next to her, looking out over the very park that'd tried to kill them. Well, to be fair, it'd had a hand. Damn it, why did he have to look so put together when her entire world felt like it was closing in on her? "I'm here. You can talk to me or not, but I'm here."

"Santa's hotline it is." Tearing her hand away from her scar, she folded her arms across her chest. Stars and ripples of the Milky Way swept across the velvet blackness above them. Out here, light pollution couldn't reach them, almost making her feel as if she were part of the universe.

He slid his hands into his sweatpants pockets. "I'm sorry. About before. In the tent. I shouldn't have—"

"If you tell me kissing me was a mistake, I will give you a firsthand look at my emotional support knife collection." They were pocketknives from all over the country and spanned decades, starting with her dad's knife from when he'd been a kid, but Branch didn't need to know that. "What's so wrong with kissing me anyway? I brushed my teeth. I got all the dirt and blood out."

His laugh only served to piss her off more. "There was nothing wrong with kissing you, Lila. Hell, I... I enjoyed it."

"Then what is it?" Now she was on a roll. That internal ball of fire she'd managed to mask with glitter and lip gloss and faux happiness had reached its capacity. "I've been nice to you since day one. I've tried to be your friend. I asked you to movies and lunch and coffee. I tried to make you laugh. I shared my Cherry Garcia with you, but none of it's good enough, is it? Nothing I do will ever be good enough, and I'm just...tired, Branch. I'm done. I give up. You win. Congratulations, you've successfully pushed everyone who gives a damn about you away."

She moved to retreat to the tent. She couldn't take this anymore. Wishing he would notice her, accept her. Want her. At some point she had to read the writing on the wall.

She only made it a few steps before strong hands spun her into his chest. His expression softened in the light of a full moon as his gaze ping-ponged between her eyes. His voice was nothing more than a whisper but was still so loud out here in the middle of nowhere. "Is that what you think? That you're not good enough for me?"

What was she supposed to say? That she really was that pathetic? That would really send him running in the other direction. No death threats or cute quips came to mind under his intensity, so she said nothing. She let him assume whatever he wanted.

His thumb brushed along her neck, over the numb scar tissue she never meant for him to see, and her stupid vagina started screaming for attention all over again. "Tell me how you got this scar."

"Telling you won't change anything." It was much harder to breathe when he was touching her like this, like he cared. She darted her tongue across her dry lips, and his gaze honed in on the small movement, signaling the rest of her body to note how close he'd gotten. Silence became a physical force between them, and she'd lost energy to keep fighting him the minute she'd escaped that too-small tent. "It'll just make things worse."

His thumb skimmed along her jaw, back and forth, back and forth. Hypnotic and soothing. "How so?"

But a flood of emotion still lightninged from her forehead to her toes as she realized what he was really asking for. He wanted everything under the sarcasm and self-deprecating humor. Under the pink kerchiefs and sweet perfume. Past the hot pink jewels on her belt and the boot laces she'd special ordered. He wanted the real her, and that right there was more terrifying than facing off with the killer's gun. "You'll see how broken I really am."

Hesitation interrupted his path along her jaw, but to his credit, he recovered quickly. "Show me."

Had he earned the right to know? Branch had searched for her after the landslide, he'd pushed himself to his limits with a head injury to save her from Sarah Lantos's killer. He'd risked his life for hers.

It would be better to finally break the fantasy of them being something more than coworkers once and for all. She owed herself that much. Lila forced her attention back to the night sky and how the tops of the cliffs met that endless velvet, grounded by his touch. "I didn't lie to you before. This scar... I did it myself. I used a knife from my collection. That's why it's so messy. The blade was dull. It took a few tries to do any damage."

"Why on earth would you do this, Lila?" His voice sounded pained, as though she'd physically stabbed him in the chest with the very same knife she'd taken to her own skin.

Her heartbeat thudded too hard at her throat, and she was sure he could feel it in his palm. "Because I deserved it."

Chapter Twenty

There was no way he'd heard her right. She'd deserved it? No one as sweet and innocent as Lila Jordan could deserve this kind of damage. Especially delivered at her own hand.

Branch swept his thumb along the ridge of her scar, memorizing every pucker, every dip. But it was the anguish in her expression that held him captive. "I can't imagine that's true."

"You're wrong." Her tongue darted across her mouth again. A nervous habit he'd noticed in the past few minutes. A coping mechanism meant to distract her brain from oncoming pain, and Branch could do nothing but hold her here in the present. "When I was seventeen, my sister and brother-in-law lost their house. He'd been fired from his job and couldn't seem to get his foot in the door anywhere else. They had to move into my parents' house, but they didn't want to be down in the basement away from everyone, so I volunteered to move into the room downstairs."

Branch had to make a conscious effort not to tighten his hold around her neck as her voice turned disconnected. His breath became rougher, jagged shards of air cutting into the soft tissues in his chest. She was standing right in front of him, and yet she felt a million miles away.

"I'd always been on good terms with my brother-in-law. We joked around, you know. Like brothers and sisters were supposed to. We hit the movies and watched soccer. I'd never had a brother before. It was fun. At first." Her voice wavered, and he couldn't help but hold his breath at the change. Usual permanent smile lines smoothed over, and right then, Branch didn't recognize the woman in front of him. "My sister worked full-time to try to get them back on their feet. She mostly worked nights as an ER nurse. Her schedule was all over the place, so my brother-in-law was around a lot while he was applying to jobs, and I just had school, so I was home most nights. It was just him and me a lot of times while my parents lived their own lives, but after a couple weeks, something changed."

An edge of concern singed his nerves. As much as he craved to learn all the little things that made Lila tick rather than the perceptions of what everyone else believed, he had no intention of retraumatizing her, of making her live through what was obviously a topic she hadn't shared with anyone. His mouth dried as quickly as the desert around them. "Lila, you don't have to—"

Her eyes raised to his. "He started sending me texts."

His intuition kicked in, but he wouldn't jump to conclusions with her again. He wouldn't let anyone or anything tarnish the free spirit digging her nails into his forearms. It took more effort than it should have to ask his next question. "What kind of texts?"

"The kind a brother-in-law shouldn't be sending his sister-in-law, or a minor." Lila sucked her lips into her mouth. Her jaw clenched, meaning she was biting down. Hard. "I never responded. I thought he was just playing some kind of sick joke on me that I didn't get, but the longer I ignored him, the worse it got. There were demands. Pictures he'd taken of himself shirtless, sometimes pantsless. Videos while he..." She shook her head as though she could burn the images from her mind. "One night, I woke up with a hand pressed over my mouth and his weight on top of me. I was so sure I'd locked the door, but he somehow got into my room. And he...forced himself on me. Multiple times."

Removing his hand from her throat altogether, Branch put some much needed space between them as the rage he'd kindled since his divorce took hold. And he couldn't take it out on her, would never forgive himself for hurting her. Devastation contorted her features, and his still-healing heart cracked all over again. The muscles in his jaw ached under the pressure of his back teeth, and all he could see was red. "Then what?"

Tears glittered in her eyes, and he felt like such an asshole right then for not being able to hold her the way she deserved. But it was too much. The violence that he wanted to inflict was on the brink of taking control, and he had no business coming within a foot of her.

"He threatened to hurt my sister if I told anyone, but the bruises... My mom noticed them. She walked in on me changing after one of my soccer games. I told her everything." Lila wrapped her arms around herself, like it took everything in her not to fall into a million pieces right here in the middle of the desert, and Branch couldn't keep his distance. Adding his strength to hers. Tremors wracked her upper body, and he only wanted to hold her tighter. Setting his forehead against hers, he took an exaggerated deep breath in an attempt to help her remain grounded.

Closing her eyes, Lila rolled her lips between her teeth. "She didn't believe me. Thought I'd made it all up to get the attention they'd been paying to my sister. Of course, my dad found out. Then my sister. My brother-in-law denied everything. I showed them the texts he'd sent, but it didn't matter. I was a seventeen-year-old girl who'd played pranks on my family from the time I could talk."

He...hadn't expected that, and a visceral red coated his vision. The only thing keeping him from marching back to headquarters and getting his hands on the name of the man who'd done this to her was the near-death grip she kept by fisting his shirt in her hands.

"I got kicked out of my house. I came home from school and found all my stuff on the front lawn." Lila stared past his shoulder to the great expanse of sky above, but her voice had lost some of its strength. "I pounded on the front door for hours, trying to get them to listen to me. Begged them to believe me. My mother answered after a while, and I thought she'd finally see the truth."

Branch's gut tightened. And then his heart broke all over again. Only it wasn't for himself this time. It was entirely for her, for the betrayal and the loss and the hurt she'd endured to get this far. "But she hadn't."

"She told me I wasn't her daughter anymore. That I needed to leave and never come back and that I was destroying our family." Her gaze slid back to his, but Lila wasn't really there. This was a ghost. Not the Ranger Barbie persona she'd created. Not the woman he'd glimpsed at Angel's Landing. He didn't know this person. She was a disassociated stranger. "I didn't find out until a few months later that my father started drinking after that. The alcohol... He took it out on my mom. My sister and brother-in-law had to move in with his parents, but she filed for divorce a few weeks later. I'd get text messages from her. Nasty things I never thought my sister would say to me."

She looked at him as though he could fight these demons for her, and Branch wanted nothing more than to drive them back, but that wasn't how reality worked. "My dad died in a drunk driving accident. He didn't have any savings or retirement after spending it all on booze, so my mom lost the house. She had to stay with one of her sisters. In the end, I think she was right. I destroyed our family."

"No, you didn't." Branch bent at the knees, putting her in his line of sight. The rage kindling under his skin took a back seat to the blatant pain in her expression. "None of what happened was your fault, Lila. The fault lies with your brother-in-law. He put you in that position. He put his hands on you. He hurt you. No one else."

"It doesn't matter, though, does it? My family wants nothing to do with me, even to this day." She shook her head, a little more awareness coming back into her blue eyes the longer he held onto her. "One of my friend's parents took me in. They made sure I had food and a roof over my head until I graduated high school, but it was never the same. There was always this…hole in my chest where my family was supposed to be. It's still there. Making it hard to breathe."

Tilting her head, Lila nonverbally begged him to ease that emptiness, and he could do nothing but trace her jaw with as much understanding as he could manage. Because he knew this pain, too. "My mom was supposed to help me shop for a prom dress. My parents were supposed to cheer for me as I crossed the stage to get my diploma. They were going to help me with college applications, and I'd planned on throwing my sister a baby shower once she got pregnant, but all of it was suddenly gone. Just gone."

Branch had never felt more connected to her than right in that moment. He felt that same hole resonate in his chest as she brought hers into the light. One soul, two bodies. Hadn't Plato or Socrates been one of the first ones to describe soulmates that way? Once whole before being rent in two by Zeus, leaving humankind to wander in loneliness and longing, searching for their other half. The way his body had tuned to hers so quickly, the way he hadn't been able to ignore her or keep his distance from the beginning despite his best efforts, how her voice and her smile resonated with him on a cellular level. No one had affected him the way she had, not even the woman he'd spent his entire adult life with up until the divorce.

He skimmed his thumb across her bottom lip, loving the way his calluses caught against the soft skin. "I'm sorry. For all of it, Lila." But none of this explained how she'd come to the point where her only option was a way out of this life at her own hand. "You blame yourself for your dad's death. Your mom's problems. Your sister's marriage. Is that why you tried to end your life?"

"Wouldn't you?" She swiped at her face with a half laugh that didn't hold an ounce of humor. She'd found her way back into the present, with him, and hell, he'd never seen a more perfect creature in his life. Strong, resilient and so damn beautiful it hurt to look at her and not touch. "I could've told my mom the bruises were from soccer. I could've deleted the messages my brother-in-law sent. I could've prevented all of this. Maybe then they would still love me. Maybe someone else could love me, too, broken pieces and all."

Shit. He wanted to be that someone. The person who could gather up all her pieces and put her back together. Stronger than ever before. Branch skimmed his hands down her arms, careful of the bullet graze on her arm. There was a reason his ex-wife had cheated on him, left him, divorced him. He wasn't good enough for Lila, and it'd never been clearer than right this moment. "Most nights I ask myself what I could've done differently in my marriage. What would've happened if I'd been a little more attentive? Was there a single moment where she fell out of love with me, or was it a lot of moments put together that went over my head?"

Forcing a deep breath, he sank into the feeling of Lila. The way she looked to him for answers, for safety. He might've gotten her out of that cave, but he'd failed her in other ways, and right then, he wasn't sure he could ever be the man she needed. The one she deserved. "I think it's natural, to take on some responsibility for the circumstances we find ourselves in, but we tend to blame ourselves for the bad while forgetting to give ourselves credit for the good."

He swept his thumb along her arm. "You're not broken, Lila. I see you. You're everything."

Chapter Twenty-One

I see you.

It was exactly what she'd wanted to hear, yet Lila hadn't been prepared for the full impact of the words. Her bones felt too big for her body, heart still thundering after Branch had led her back to the tent last night and tucked her into his chest. Safe. Accepted. Supported. Where she'd always wanted to be. He had a power over her that would be death of her. Because when he talked to her like that, when he held her and comforted her after spilling her darkest secrets, she could almost believe the man of her dreams—and countless fantasies—wanted her in return.

Ugh. Why did she have to be so...broken?

Why couldn't she accept maybe he had meant everything he said last night? And why couldn't she stop staring at the ceiling of the tent as if it held all the answers?

"I know you're awake." His voice was gravelly, deeper than usual, and her lady bits were the first to take notice. Holy moly, the man could do some damage with few words.

Branch pressed his chest against her back, shoulder to knee, though he was so much bigger than her. She loved it, this sudden need for him to get as close as possible, despite a whole lot of reasons why he shouldn't. Number one: morning breath. His hand slid over her hip, across her low belly, and she wanted nothing more than to melt into him. To forget all the bad outside these crappy canvas walls and live out one of the fantasies she'd built in her head. Years of therapy had gotten her to a place of being able to hold her own in any given situation with a man, but there was something visceral that convinced her survival instincts that Branch wouldn't ever hurt her.

"Your stomach announced your presence before the rest of you stirred."

Traitor. Her stomach vaulted into her chest as Branch planted a kiss on her shoulder. Forget butterflies. An entire Cirque du Soleil act had started up behind her ribs. While they'd done nothing more than share that one kiss and fall asleep in each other's arms last night, Branch Thompson had made her feel a whole lot of dangerous things that scared the crap out of her.

Pushing her upper body off the unyielding ground, Lila added a few inches of breathing room between them. Didn't help. Because looking at his face first thing in the morning was suddenly all she wanted to do with the rest of her life. "You're one to talk. I fell asleep to an entire orchestra performing in your intestines."

Okay. Those words were not sexy. At all.

But his laugh sure as hell was. It filled the tent with a warmth the sun couldn't touch as it crawled over the horizon. His touch fell from her hip as he rolled onto his back.

"Touché." Muscles flexed across his stomach and chest as he hauled himself upright. And what an impressive show it was. In fact, Morning Branch just might be the new star of her unachievable fantasies from here on out.

If this whole investigation left her—and her heart—in one piece. "I'll get us some breakfast."

Yeah. There was little chance of getting out of this without more bruises.

They'd lost track of the killer and the gun that could've killed her, but Lila knew in her heart the hunt wasn't over. The man who'd killed Sarah Lantos might've convinced himself of his heroic role in this mess, but that didn't mean he deserved to get away with murder. One way or another, NPS was going to find him, and she wanted to be there when they did.

Grabbing her pack, she kept her attention on changing back into her uniform rather than watching the way Branch had jumped at the opportunity to feed her. No one had really done that for her. Sure, her parents made sure she'd been fed as a kid, but once she'd hit ten or eleven, her mother had taught her to cook her own meals apart from dinner. Even then, her mom had made it seem like feeding the family was more a burden than anything else. None of her past boyfriends—however few and far between—had made the effort to ensure she ate. Rather, they'd expected her to feed them. But Branch... He was taking care of her.

And maybe that was the scariest part of all. She'd gone so long taking care of herself, she wasn't sure how to let someone else do it. And that kiss? Wow. It'd been deep and slow, and oh so intense, she was still feeling it in her nerve endings. His touch, his weight—all of it combined into a dangerous cocktail. That kiss had whispered promises of something she'd dreamed about since she'd met him. It promised forever, but she and Branch didn't have that. Not with the gaping wounds she'd exposed.

The smell of cinnamon and apples hit her a split second

before Branch offered a small plastic bowl and a spoon. "Can't say it's as satisfying as Cherry Garcia, but oatmeal should hold us over until we reach headquarters in a few hours."

Right. All this was temporary. The real world wouldn't wait forever. Soon or later, search and rescue would set out to see what had become of them, and she and Branch would have to give their statements about the past twenty-four hours. And explain why they'd failed to hold onto Sarah Lantos's killer. She could see Risner's winning smile now—part hyena, part snake—as he found the last reason he needed to dismiss her from the service. Ugh. Lila stared down into the over-sugared mush in her bowl and closed her eyes. "I will not stab him for talking about ice cream. I will not stab him for talking about ice cream."

"Not a morning person." Branch settled himself on his sleeping bag as she peeled open her eyes. It was admirable the way he tried to fold his legs crisscross-applesauce with his size, but there didn't seem to be any obstacle that held its strength against him. Especially her ovaries. "Noted."

Her heart hiccuped. He said that as if he planned to wake up next to her after today, which was just straight-up ridiculous, but if he could read her mind, he would either be traumatized or turned on. Both, if he was as awesome as she believed him to be.

They'd return to headquarters, Risner would fire her, she'd pack her crap as Sayles looked on, and she'd never see Branch or any of the other rangers again. They'd get what they'd wanted since she started working in Zion: a great view of her ass on the way out. The end. She swallowed the groan in the back of her throat along with a chunk of apple.

"If you don't terrify people a little bit, then what's the

point of all of this?" Shoveling oatmeal into her mouth—and not thinking about the two pints of Ben & Jerry's in her freezer in her soon-to-be former shoebox of a house—Lila finished off breakfast and shoved her hands into her uniform top over her sleep shirt. The less they dragged this out, the better. Then again, she never could rip off a Band-Aid without crying.

Within a few minutes, Branch had cleaned and packed their dishware. They each rolled and stored their sleeping bags with a mental inventory of the supplies they had left between them. It wasn't much, but the hike back to headquarters shouldn't take more than five hours if they kept a steady pace, though their injuries would add some time.

The sky had darkened some since she'd woken, but it wasn't until Lila shouldered her pack that she caught a whiff of rain in the air. Storm clouds had started gathering in the north, bringing a gust of frigid wind. She hadn't packed any long-sleeved protection.

Branch followed her gaze on the incoming clouds. They were moving in fast, rolling over each other and bringing nothing but dread. "Let's move."

The banter they'd shared evaporated as the wind picked up, rocketing her nerves higher. It wasn't as though they weren't trained to survive in severe weather. Both she and Branch had gone through hours of wilderness survival before signing on with NPS. They both knew the potential of getting wet and suffering hypothermia despite the summer temperatures. Additionally, search and rescue would call off any attempts made to recover her and Branch due to the storm.

Lila caught the briefest flash of lightning in her peripheral vision, and soon a backing track of thunder ricocheted off the surrounding cliffs. The hairs along her arms raised on end, driving her up the bowl-like incline of the valley.

Her legs screamed protest with every step, her bruised ribs limiting her breathing. She'd never met a mountain she couldn't conquer during her reign as a park ranger, but this little molehill would be her undoing. Not to mention the fantastic view of Branch's backside on the way up. But she had to slow down. Her body had yet to recover its run-in with a landslide and a killer, and it was showing. "What fresh hell is this?"

"Almost there. Come on." Reaching back for her, Branch intertwined his fingers with hers, pulling her to his side. He kept one hand at her low back, and his warmth instantly assaulted the nerves scraping up her spine. Then it was gone. "I've got you."

"You say that now, but four of the five voices in my head think you're too good to be true, and the fifth is deciding where to bury you." She sucked down a deep breath tinged with humidity that hadn't been there a moment ago. Rain was coming.

She was gifted another one of his laughs, but this one didn't have any feeling to it. Not like the one back in the tent. Still, she couldn't help but engrave it into her brain for recall later when he finally realized she wasn't worth the effort. Or maybe he already had.

Static punctured through the silence between them, right before a low voice sounded over Lila's radio. "Thompson, Jordan, come in. Over." Another round of static.

Lila pulled up short, unthreading her arm from one shoulder strap, and pulled her pack forward. They'd reached the rim of the valley, but the mountains and the incoming storm should've kept them from contacting headquarters. Unless help was closer than she thought. Pulling her beaten radio from the pack, she clamped down the push-to-talk button as Branch took position in front of her. "Jordan here. Risner, is that you?"

Two seconds. Three.

"Jordan, it's about time. Where's Branch?" Cold slithered through her at the district ranger's instant demand to talk to someone who wasn't her.

"He's here. We're approximately three miles northeast from the base of Angel's Landing and headed back." Apart from the very real possibility of not having a job when they returned to headquarters, she couldn't deny the relief of knowing someone had been searching for them. "Over."

"Stay put. We're a mile out from you, and I want answers. Seismometers picked up a reading eighteen hours ago, but the geologists are telling me it wasn't an earthquake." Risner's voice cut out on the last word. "What the hell is going on out there? Over."

A mile? Another dose of dread prickled in her gut. This was it. Once SAR recovered her and Branch, they'd be separated to give their statements, she'd be dismissed from NPS, and all of this would be over.

Lila struggled to respond. The past twenty-four hours had changed her in ways she couldn't explain. For better and worse. And Branch had been there through it all, but she'd known—deep down—this fantasy she'd created between them hadn't ever been a real possibility from the beginning. It was only a matter of time before he realized how much work it would take to put her back together, and he'd barely made it out of his divorce in one piece. His heart couldn't afford another bond with the wrong soul. And she was…wrong. In every way.

Taking the radio from her, Branch lifted it to his mouth,

his attention locked on her. "Ranger Jordan ensured we got out alive. Other than that, we're going to need additional rangers to aid in the search. Over."

Lila's lips parted on a strong inhale. Oh, no. Branch Thompson had taken her entire heart, and she was pretty sure he'd never give it back.

Chapter Twenty-Two

Something had changed. In the span of a mere twenty-four hours, Branch had been cracked wide open all over again. Only this time, the pieces were coming together without the need of isolation, hiding or avoidance. All because of the woman standing in front of him.

She'd washed her face free of makeup, leaving nothing but the imperfect beauty beneath. Hair frizzing free from the ponytail she'd dragged it into, Lila stood against the backdrop of thunder and lightning and the promise of torrential summer rain. And, damn it, she was perfect. Her uniform had worn through over her ribs, revealing her sleep shirt underneath where bruises darkened smooth skin, and in an instant, he recalled the feeling of the fabric between his fingers. Recalled how his palm had fit perfectly against her hip, those little breathy sounds she made in her sleep, the guttural moan as he'd kissed her last night. He'd fallen asleep to the rhythmic rise and fall of her back pressed against his chest, and it'd been the most peaceful night's sleep he'd gotten in years.

Hell. He could still taste her. A driving, ravenous need to kiss her—to absorb her into his very bones—sucked the oxygen from his lungs, and Branch pushed himself to add another foot of distance between them. He prided himself on discipline, on control, but everything about this woman urged him to discard every stupid rule he'd set in place to protect himself. The mere thought terrified him beyond facing Sarah Lantos's killer.

A smile caught at one corner of her mouth, sending an SOS straight to his nervous system as she studied him. But even with as much as she'd revealed about herself last night—the assault, her parents' reaction, her attempt to take her own life—he couldn't rid himself of the feeling there was something Lila had left out. That he was being left in the dark.

That same feeling had been there in the days leading up to catching his ex-wife with his best friend, then afterward when his ex had admitted she was going to seek an abortion. It burned low in his stomach, acidic and uncomfortable. But what could Lila possibly have to keep from him? They were rangers, had worked together for a mere four months. They'd only recently crossed the line into something akin to friends—maybe more—and there wasn't a single cell in his body that believed she owed him a damn thing.

Unless it had something to do with this investigation.

Shit. That thought shot his brain into hyperawareness, assessing every interaction they'd had over the past two days and deconstructing the meaning behind every word out of her perfect mouth. The paranoia and betrayal he'd shoved in a box made of rage burst free, and in an instant, he was in too deep, drowning. On the verge of putting himself right back where he didn't want to be: at the mercy of someone he trusted.

Lila dragged her ponytail over her shoulder and twisted the ends between slender fingers tipped in that chipping manicure. He wasn't sure how long she'd been hiding underneath all the pink and rhinestones, but it would take months, if not years, to crawl out from the persona she'd built to shield herself from judgment, hurt and backstabbings. She'd need support. She'd need him with her every step of the way, but she didn't trust him. "I'm not sure anyone has ever stood up to Risner and lived to tell the tale."

His mouth dried. Thunder exploded overhead as the clouds moved in. The first rain drops pattered against his scalp and shoulders, and Lila, in all her glory, stared up into the sky as if daring the torrent to do its worst. She closed her eyes against the onslaught without a care in the world.

And wasn't that kindling to the fire raging inside of him? That she could go through life relying on her impulsiveness, her emotions and meddling without bothering to acknowledge the consequences? How did she get a pass when everyone else had to pay the price for their choices?

Somehow this woman had crawled beneath layers of armor and made herself at home as though she owned the place, and damn it, he was pretty sure she owned him. After everything she'd been through—everything she'd suffered—she'd managed to bury it all with a smile, cheer for her enemies and push back despite the odds.

But it'd all been a lie. A manipulation.

And if he took that step to keep her, she would only end up breaking him completely. Branch fisted both hands to stop himself from reaching for her, to feel her rain-slickened skin and wipe the drops from her lips with his mouth. This resilient creature had shown him what life without pain could look like. Shown him how to feel comfortable in his skin and move on while driving his invisible knife wounds deeper.

The muscles in his jaw ached under the pressure of his back teeth as he surveyed the storm overhead. To keep himself from memorizing her all over again. Or witnessing Lila break from what had to come next. "Why did Sarah Lantos's killer want you dead?"

"Well, you sure know how to make a girl feel special." Lila's smile slipped as she opened her eyes to study him. Rain plastered her hair against her face, and Branch's fingers itched to set it back behind her ear. To have one last touch. But it would only make this so much harder on both of them. Her mouth parted on a rough exhale, and she diverted her attention to the ridgeline where the SAR unit would approach from. As if hoping they would intervene and save her this conversation. That was only one the red flags Branch noted. "I don't presume to know the inner workings of murderers, but I'm guessing I was standing in his way."

The lie shoved a bitter, acidic sensation up his throat. "Then why didn't he just kill you? Why drag you to his campsite?"

"I told you." Dropping her hands away from her hair, she squared her shoulders to him. "Sarah Lantos fought back. He needed me to patch up a stab wound to his thigh. You were there, weren't you? Didn't you see the bloodied gauze?"

Yeah. He had, and it'd driven him nearly out of his mind imagining Lila had been injured. That her abductor was trying to save her life, but it'd turned out, she'd been trying to save his. Branch took that step forward, more determined than ever to uncover what she was hiding. "But you ran. And he followed, even with a stab wound and the risk of bleeding out. He could've just shot you. He had the gun. Why did he chase you down? Why follow you into that cave?"

"Branch, don't do this." Her eyes widened, begging

him to back off, and right then, he knew. He knew there was something she hadn't told him about the man they were hunting.

"Why did he want you dead, Ranger Jordan?" Using her title and last name suddenly made it far easier for him to keep his emotions out of this, and physical pain registered on her face. A flinch of the worst kind. Was that why Risner insisted on calling his female rangers by their last names? To distance himself from giving a damn about them? Maybe the man wasn't sexist, after all. Maybe he'd just learned to not to get emotionally involved.

No, that guy was still an asshole.

The rain picked up, but it did nothing to mask the swell of tears in her eyes or the sweet scent of her skin. Her tongue darted across her bottom lip. Only this time Branch wouldn't let himself get taken in. "He said I was just like her. Sarah Lantos. That I deserved to suffer for manipulating people into doing what I wanted by convincing them I was something I wasn't. Is that what you want to hear?"

His gut somersaulted, and he countered his advance. Her lie had been right there, staring him in the face, but he'd refused to let himself see it because of the feelings she'd stirred in him. "You lied to me. When I asked, you told me you didn't remember anything else from the cave."

"I didn't..." She shook her head, then stilled. Branch watched as she connected the dots. Realized her mistake and what it meant. Lila took a step forward but halted as he took one back. Her face drained of color, voice softening. "I didn't mean to lie to you, I swear. I just—"

"You just what? After everything I told you about my ex-wife, you ended up being just like her, didn't you? Willing to do whatever it takes to get your way at the cost of the people around you. I trusted you to be up front with me, but you may have just compromised this investigation. The killer's motives can tell us about the types of victims he targets or his next move. That information might've given us a clue as to where he's going, and you kept it to yourself because, what? You didn't want to confirm what everyone else already knows?" Branch didn't wait for an answer, stalking past her. He was well aware he was searching for an excuse to sever this gut-wrenching need for her out of fear, but he couldn't afford to risk his heart again. Ending it now was the only way to protect himself, no matter how much he hated himself for it. "Wait here for the search party, Ranger Jordan. Tell Risner I'm still on the killer's trail."

"You can't go out there alone. Branch, please. You're not in any condition to face him again." Threading her hand between his arm and rib cage, she fought to stop him in his tracks.

He turned on her with every ounce of disgust he could muster in his expression.

She dropped her hold as if she'd been burned. Her throat worked on a deep swallow. "I'm sorry. Okay? I didn't want you to think I was that person he accused me of being, the one everyone accuses me of being. I can't lose you, too."

"Too late." Branch lowered his voice, hating himself more than ever before. "Were you even telling the truth about that scar, or was it another way for you to get attention? To make me and the other rangers feel bad for you?"

The words achieved the impact he'd wanted. He'd used her mother's accusations against her, and Branch couldn't help but feel he'd gone too far.

"You said you see me." Her voice barely reached him

over the storm throwing her hair in her face. "That I'm not broken."

This was how he ended it. How he kept what'd happened leading to his divorce from happening again. Every muscle in his body stiffened with self-hatred, but he'd already made the jump. He had to see this through to the end. "I was wrong."

It took less than three seconds for Ranger Barbie to make an appearance, and he couldn't stand to watch her rebuild those impenetrable walls. "You've exceeded the limits of my medication. So enjoy your next twenty-four hours, Branch Thompson."

Lila turned on her heel, soaked to the bone, and headed in the direction of Angel's Landing. Never one to follow orders. Then again, he'd liked that about her. Her penchant for doing whatever the hell she wanted had put her on his radar in the first place and secured her position in the investigation into Sarah Lantos's murder. But now... now his gut warned him not to let her trudge through the desert during an increasingly violent storm alone. Without his protection.

But hadn't that been the point? To add this distance—physically and emotionally—between them? So why didn't he feel better about his decision?

He dug his fingertips into his palms to stop himself from calling after her. Risner would intercept her in the next few minutes. She'd return to headquarters, give her statement of the past two days and go back to the way things were supposed to be. And he'd...move on. Once and for all.

Branch couldn't go back. Ever. He couldn't see her patrolling the park every day and not want to get a dose of that smile she seemingly reserved for him or show up at her front door with a couple pints of Cherry Garcia and a romantic comedy from the 2000s.

No. He was going to finish what he started by ensuring the killer didn't come for Lila again.

Chapter Twenty-Three

He'd given her the one thing she'd wanted most. And then he'd taken it away as though it meant nothing.

Lila's boots slogged through mud and puddles, getting sucked down into the earth with every forced step forward. Cold rain slapped against her face but did nothing to cool her rising body temperature, prickles punctuating the vile words circling her head.

She couldn't breathe properly, couldn't think of anything other than the pure disgust written all over Branch's face as he'd accused her of being the very thing so many others had. A joke, a tease, a liar. Her heart broke all over again as she followed the valley's upper rim. Reds, oranges and tans bled together through the tears in her eyes. She hadn't lied to him. She hadn't. Omitting what the killer had said to her had been nothing but an attempt to convince herself how wrong he'd been. Instead, she'd ended up hurting the one person she'd trusted.

Branch had every reason to despise her. After what happened with his ex-wife, she didn't blame him for shutting her out. Lies of omission were still lies, and there was nothing she could do—nothing she could say—to fix this. No matter how much she wanted to. She'd done exactly as she'd feared. She'd manipulated him into believing she was something she wasn't. A magician, as the killer had called her, and she never felt so alone.

An all-too-familiar, sickening twist cut through her stomach. Lila slapped her hand against the nearest rock wall and emptied her stomach of the oatmeal Branch had made her this morning. How had everything gone wrong in such a short amount of time? How could she have let herself screw this up after everything she'd been through with her family? Wasn't she supposed to learn from her mistakes? She'd had everything she wanted. And now...

She felt as though she was sinking and wished the earth would swallow her whole right here. Her heart pounded loud in her ears to the point not even the breaking thunder overhead could penetrate through the haze. The storm seemed to mimic the suffering inside, which only drove her deeper into the spiral.

Her knuckles ached as though she'd spent the past few hours pounding on a bright yellow door that would never welcome her again. Begging to be let in, for someone—anyone—to believe she didn't deserve this.

But she did, didn't she?

A sob broke free of her throat, and Lila heaved again until there was nothing left. Rejection and bile left her mouth sticky and dry, but she wouldn't unpack her water bottle. She deserved to sit in this emptiness, to taste nothing but ash on her tongue for the rest of her life. To go back to being that seventeen-year-old unlovable girl no one wanted.

Her mother had been right all along. Losing Branch proved it, didn't it? There was nothing she could do—no one she could be—that would make anyone want her. Her brother-in-law had destroyed her, ripped away her sense of self and broken it into a million tiny pieces that could never be recovered. ——— nothing. Unimportant, overlooked. Not even pretending to be the bubbly, enthusiastic cheerleader who loved pink and meeting up for coffee convinced people to give her a chance.

Lila swiped her mouth with her hand and sank her back into the cliffside. Rain soaked through her hair and smeared down her face, anything but cleansing. A shiver chased across her shoulders as lightning struck overhead. Risner and the search and rescue team should be here any minute, but as she took in the towering cliffs overhead, she realized she must've taken a wrong turn in her desperation to put as much distance between her and Branch as possible. Damn it. There was no way the SAR team would find her unless she got back on the main path to Angel's Landing. Right then, she felt as airheaded as her fellow rangers believed her to be.

Peeling herself away from the rock face, she trudged back the way she came, following her own treads as a guide. Her throat hurt. Her head hurt. Her heart…hurt.

Branch had effectively drawn her in with promises of understanding and desire and something more and then crushed that hope with nothing more than a few words. Bitterness coated her tongue, and no amount of swallowing got rid of the taste. He'd accused her of trying to kill herself all those years ago to get attention. Just as her mother had before excommunicating her from the family, all the while messaging her photos of herself and her son-in-law going out to lunch together, catching movies together, meeting for coffee.

She'd wanted that. So much. To the point she'd tried to recreate it with her fellow rangers, but something must be…wrong with her. All she'd wanted was someone to choose her, and she'd almost convinced herself Branch had been that person. Her person, but he'd stabbed her heart instead. Used her greatest shame against her and successfully killed off the last shards of hope she'd held onto all these years. Tears burned in her eyes, though she tried to breathe around them. She wasn't sure she could ever forgive him for that. "If karma doesn't kill him, I gladly will."

No. She couldn't hurt him. Not the way he'd hurt her. Despite the hollowness taking up more space than it had before, a part of her had been dedicated to him since the moment he stepped into Zion. Had fallen in love with him. And that was what hurt the most. Her crush had become something…more over the past few days. Not the numb never-going-to-happen fantasy she'd lived off of. She'd shared trauma with him, shared a bed with him. She'd fallen asleep in his arms and given him a glimpse of the darkness she'd carried. She'd imagined a future with him, trusted him. He'd made her feel alive in a way no search and rescue or climbing assignment or hyperfixation had.

But she tended to overreact to anyone who showed her the slightest hint of kindness. That was what trauma did. It brought her expectations of human decency so low, that even wishing "bless you" after a sneeze urged her to sign over her savings in gratitude.

And she could see now that'd she handed over the most sacred parts of herself to Branch because he'd pulled her out of that cave. He'd saved her life. And while it made sense for her to offer something in return, she'd allowed herself to forget the months of growls, annoyed glances and one-sided conversations between them. He'd made it clear from the beginning, hadn't he? He'd wanted nothing to do with her since day one, and yet she'd somehow ended up giving him everything that mattered. "Now I get to fill his bed with Nature's Valley granola bars."

Lila stepped back onto the main trail that would lead her to the base of Angel's Landing. The search and rescue team's position didn't matter in this storm. They would hunker down until the worst passed, which, judging by the way the wind had picked up and thunder exploded overhead, would be a while yet. She'd get out of here faster—away from Branch sooner—by meeting the team where they were now.

A warning teased at the back of her mind. She knew better than to trek the park alone in the middle of a storm like this, but the need to get back to her crappy little house, eat a crappy lunch of ice cream and pack her crappy belongings drove her along the trail. The truth was, even if Risner somehow didn't dismiss her from the NPS or reassign her to another park, she wasn't going back. There was no way she could face Branch on the trails or in staff meetings or in the break room after he'd used her deepest regret against her.

And explaining this all to Sayles... That just wasn't going to happen. Her roommate had her own life, her own person in the form of an FBI agent who melted anytime he set eyes on Sayles, and Lila wasn't going to mess with that. "And this is why you never date anyone from work."

Her fingertips brushed the scar across her neck. The skin tingled there as she recalled Branch's touch, how he'd been so gentle and caring when he'd asked her to tell him what'd happened. How he'd held her as she exposed every nasty detail of an event that had turned her into a fraud.

But she didn't know him. Not really.

The man she'd come to know these past two days never would've accused her of using this scar for attention. But then maybe she hadn't really known him at all. Growls, rejection after rejection and negotiating shifts that didn't involve her had kind of made it hard.

Didn't matter. Once she met up with the search and rescue team, she'd give Risner her notice, and Branch Thompson would be nothing more than another rhinestone on her mud-caked belt.

The rain washed her boot prints from the mud ahead, but another set took shape. Larger, more widely spaced. She slowed, studying each one. Had the SAR team already caught up with her? The storm should keep them pinned down.

Crouching, she feathered her touch over the ridges breaking apart with each pit of rain. "No treads."

Lila stood quickly, turning back the way she'd come.

Pain erupted in her gut as the killer's outline took shape. She looked down. Watched her blood spread across her uniform from where the small knife penetrated. A hand slapped against one shoulder, holding her in place, forcing her to feel every twitch of the knife he held.

"Hello, Ranger Jordan." The killer slid the knife free of her low belly, still holding her upright. "I've been looking for you. There's still so much more for us to talk about before we were rudely interrupted."

"You." Stumbling back, Lila clutched her hand over the wound, free of his hold, but there was no stopping the blood leaking through her fingers. Her entire body swayed as the onslaught of pain intensified. It took everything she had not to compare this moment to the night of her assault, to relive it rather than stay in her head. To fight back. The heels of her boots dipped down as she met the upper rim of the valley.

"You're a liar like she was, Ranger Jordan." Sarah Lantos's killer stepped into her personal space, skimming his breath along her jawline. "And I intend to make you suffer."

One push. That was all it took for her to go over the edge.

The world tipped on its axis as she fell. Her legs dropped out from under her. Gravity sucked her down to earth as she rolled. Rocks speared into her bruised ribs and cut through the fabric of her uniform. Her hair caught in cacti and bushes and ripped free again and again, tearing chunks from her scalp. She landed at the base of the incline, flat on her stomach.

Blood filled her mouth. Rushed to her head. Thudded too hard in her chest. Stretching one arm out, Lila reached for a palm-size rock a few feet in front of her. Not to escape. She knew that was impossible, but she wouldn't make this easy for him, either. Something warm and sticky dropped into her left eye, interrupting her vision. More blood. It dripped from the same incision she'd sustained when Branch had saved her from becoming a human pancake, mixing with rain and puddling beneath her chin.

A boot pressed down onto her forearm as her fingers brushed the rock. The killer crouched beside her, crushing her arm beneath his weight. But it was nothing compared to the agony in her chest. Of knowing Branch wouldn't be coming to save her again.

"Looks like it's just you and me now, Ranger Jordan."

Chapter Twenty-Four

The rubber band around his heart snapped harder than ever before.

Branch struggled to take his next breath as he met up with the mouth of the canyon that would lead north. Lila had been right before. This was the only escape that made sense to get the killer out of the park as fast as possible and without ranger interference. It was also the most dangerous. Though he hadn't caught sight of Fluffy yet, flash floods weren't uncommon in the area. With the storm bearing down, he could get swept away without more than a few seconds' warning. There was a chance the mountain lion had sought shelter during the storm, which just went to prove how out of it Branch really was.

Or maybe he was looking to punish himself.

He couldn't stop the accusations he'd thrown at her from circling his head. Every step punctuated by another vile word. He'd accused her of lying to him. Not just about what she'd kept from him during the investigation but of using her past to manipulate him. Like her mother had. Like the other rangers had. Like the killer had.

Damn it, it was the most detestable thing he'd ever done. Worse than taking a baseball bat to his best friend's car the minute Brand caught him and his ex-wife in bed together. It'd felt good at the time—like lifting a weight he hadn't realized had been crushing him for months—but he didn't have that feeling now.

All he could think about was Lila's flinch, as though he'd physically struck her. The dullness in her eyes. The way she'd hugged herself to keep from breaking in front of him.

Branch pushed himself harder, wanting nothing more than to ease the regret churning in his gut, but the relief never came. He'd messed up. He'd taken something beautiful and delicate and crushed it the moment he got attached.

That was what he did though, wasn't it? He took and took without giving back. And then he took some more. It was why his ex-wife had started looking to his best friend for intimacy. It was why she hadn't told him about the pregnancy immediately. Why she'd made a life-changing decision without considering what he'd wanted. At some point, she'd felt he couldn't be trusted.

The moment Lila had given him her trust by telling him all the ways her family failed her and the blame she'd shouldered alone for so long, a switch had flipped. He'd shut down any part of himself that allowed emotion and connection, but with her... It'd all come rushing back.

It was as though he'd been standing outside his bedroom door, right back on the edge of that cliff, knowing one more step would change his life, and he'd been afraid of falling. Moans of pleasure puncturing through the thin wood, his hand on the cold doorknob, his heart in his throat. Out there in the middle of the desert with Lila, he'd been back at that door. One step away from claiming the support and connection he'd wanted since the divorce or retreating to safety where he didn't have to worry about corrupting another woman into resenting him. Where no one could touch him.

He'd made his choice.

Only now, Branch couldn't stop rubbing his chest. Knowing if he allowed himself to slow down, the ache would consume him from the inside. He'd survived losing the woman he'd planned on spending the rest of his life with, but this…this was different.

Somehow, deep down, he understood this pain would only get worse the more distance he added between him and Ranger Barbie. And, damn it, he deserved to live in it. To feel every twinge of agony for what he'd said to her. He wasn't good enough for a woman like Lila Jordan who put everyone else before herself, who cheered for the very people working to tear her down, who never gave up. He was hard where she was soft, demanding where she compromised, unforgiving and intolerable where she accepted every facet of his grumpy ass. And he'd thrown it all in her face out of fear. Fear of destroying every good thing that made her the beautiful creature she was.

The tug to turn back intensified until it stole his next breath. Sarah Lantos's killer had targeted Lila. It made sense for him to make sure the son of a bitch couldn't come back for his partner, but there wouldn't be a woman to save if he left things like this between them. Branch pulled up short of the very cave he'd found her cornered by the killer. He had a choice. Duty to his job and this park or choosing Lila. It wasn't much of a choice.

Turning around, he navigated the smooth riverbed, his pace picking up once he reached the mouth of the canyon. That invisible thread connecting him and Lila had grown taut, pulling him back to Angel's Landing. To her.

The valley stretched out in front of him. Lightning

struck the ground about a half mile away, raising the hairs along his forearm as he stepped out into the open. His nervous system screamed danger as he navigated forgotten boulders and exposed roots. The trees here had already burned due to a lightning strike two years ago, but that didn't mean another fire couldn't erupt without notice. The first few drops of the next storm spit against his face. His legs ached under the weight of his pack as he jogged across the expanse. Lungs on fire, Branch ignored the pounding in his head.

Seconds stretched into minutes. Minutes into hours. Every single one of them etched deep into his skin as he closed the distance between them. Lila had most likely already met up with the search and rescue team, but the storm would slow them down. He could still catch her. He'd beg for her forgiveness, then let her go if that was what she chose. It would hurt, but it was nothing short of what he deserved. To live the rest of his life alone and regretful.

The ache in his chest doubled in size, spreading like a wildfire through his arms and legs as he crested the bowl-like incline of the valley. Angel's Landing wasn't too much farther, and it would take time for the entire SAR team to ascend the cliffside leading to the lookout with their gear. Just another mile or so. His pulse thudded in rhythm to his steps as he followed the curved upper rim of the valley.

Then he saw them. The search team.

An added burst of energy shot down his legs. Within seconds, he closed in on Risner huddled under a rocky outcropping blocking out the rain, but he couldn't pick out the pink nightmare he'd been searching for in the group. Every ranger had donned their Stetsons, throwing him off, but it was clear within a few seconds that Lila wasn't among them. Had she pushed ahead?

The district ranger raised his attention, setting beady dark eyes on him. Risner's thin frame towered over the others in the team, most likely providing the supervisor with a power trip he hadn't earned. "Branch, it's about time. We've been waiting for you. What the hell is going on out here? I got reports of a landslide but no seismic activity. You know anything about that?"

"The killer used dynamite to trigger the landslide." Trying to catch his breath, Branch studied the canyons ahead, hoping to catch a glimpse of her. He'd told her to wait for the SAR team, but knowing her, she'd decided to head back to headquarters alone. Despite the fact that was where she would be safest, he couldn't help but wonder if she'd be there when he returned. "Ranger Jordan and I were caught in the fallout. We've been tracking the killer. We barely escaped with our lives. You got anything on this guy? A way to identify him?"

Risner jumped at the opportunity to take the lead. "The medical examiner concluded Sarah Lantos was dead before she hit the ground. The stab wound to her side severed the superior...mercenary artery. Something like that."

"Superior mesenteric artery." Another member of the team tossed out a tarp to set up a temporary campsite.

"Right. That. The victim bled out in seconds. The ME says the killer must've had some knowledge of anatomy or he just got lucky killing her that quickly. I'm thinking the latter, considering he's messing around with dynamite. Nobody mentally stable risks their own life with materials like that." Risner swiped the back of his hand beneath his nose to catch the water dripping off the birdlike cartilage. "The blood found on the lookout belongs to the victim. There were no traces of the killer left behind, not even on the gear and ropes. Killer must've worn gloves. Best we can tell, Sarah Lantos was in the wrong place at the wrong time."

That didn't feel right. Not after everything he and Lila had gone through. "Lila said the killer wanted Sarah Lantos to suffer, that she deserved to pay for what she'd done to him for years. She thinks this is personal to him. Did you run a background check on the victim? Does she have any priors, incidents or family members with records?"

Branch was with Lila on this. He didn't have a whole lot of experience studying motives and modes of operation, but he knew there were warning signs leading up to someone taking a life. Something that might pinpoint who'd killed the victim. And tried to kill Lila.

"She thinks this is personal, huh? Well, since your partner isn't here, we'll have to operate on the assumption the people who actually investigate homicides around here are right." Risner scanned the landscape beyond Branch's shoulders, hands on his hips as though ready to dole out long-awaited punishment for his metaphorical punching bag. "Where is Jordan, by the way? You were both supposed to wait for the SAR team."

Branch's heart stopped cold for the briefest of moments. He searched every team member's face, desperate to recognize the blue eyes he'd woken to this morning in the tent. "What do you mean? I told her to wait here to meet up with you."

"Haven't seen her." Risner angled his arms out, palms up in a shrug. "Damn woman can never do anything right. I warned you not to bring her in on this investigation, but I guess you just couldn't keep it in your pants, Thompson. Don't blame you. Jordan's got that look in her eye that says she'll do anything for attention." The district ranger lowered his voice, barely audible over the pounding rain on the tarp the others had raised. "I expect details when we get back to headquarters." Risner winked. Stepping back, he widened his stance, thumbs hooked into his belt. "We're moving out as soon as this storm passes. We can't wait for her to catch up."

"You can't just leave her out here on her own." His nervous system shot into overdrive as he closed the distance between him and Risner.

The slight widening of the district ranger's eyes told him every preconception he'd had of Branch had been wrong, that he didn't know who the hell he was dealing with. And Branch couldn't argue. He was an entirely different person from two days ago, changed in more ways than one because of a woman who enjoyed threatening to make his life hell.

"And if I ever hear you talk about an employee, especially a female employee, like that again, I'll have the superintendent ship you to Gateway Arch for the rest of your pathetic career. As for Lila never doing anything right, have you bothered to ask yourself if you're the kind of leader employees respect enough to follow orders? Because from where I'm standing, there's a lot to be desired."

Risner's jaw snapped shut as he puffed out his chest, just begging for someone to knock him down a peg. "Whether my employees respect me or not doesn't matter. I'm her superior."

"You're an idiot, and if you aren't going to make the right call to recover one of your rangers, I am." Branch hauled his pack higher on his shoulder. "I'm going after her."

Chapter Twenty-Five

Lila couldn't keep her blood where it should be. In her body. The blade hadn't hit anything major, but it was only a matter of time before she bled out if she didn't get any kind of medical help. Except she wasn't sure how to do that. Her legs weren't working. The killer had confiscated her radio. And no one—not even Branch—knew she was here.

"What do you think of my kidnapping skills now, Ranger Jordan?" That voice, tinted with a slight accent she still couldn't place, filtered in through the darkness.

Thunder rumbled up through the ground. Or had it come from above? She couldn't tell. Something sharp set up residence in her chest, shortening her inhales. Wave after wave of dizziness had tossed her brain in a blender and refused to relent. "You've got the incapacitating your victim part down. Kudos. The cave is also a great touch. Spooky."

Her throat ached with every attempt to speak, draining what energy she had left faster. Another bubble of blood burst from the wound in her stomach. Sarah Lantos had been stabbed just like this, but she imagined it would've been too much work for the killer to get Lila to the top of Angel's Landing with an injury like the one in his thigh. Which seemed to have been patched up as he approached her, discarding the shadows of whatever cave he'd dragged her into.

His laugh rolled with another explosion of thunder. Ugh. She hated that laugh. Bet it'd become the star of her nightmares after this. The storm was still going strong, but it did nothing to drown out the killer's intentions. "Thank you. I've learned a lot since the last time you and I were alone together."

"Is this the part where you open up your case of torture devices and detail your master plan while explaining how I don't fit into it?" Pain spiked through her middle as she tried to push herself upright. "Or am I part of the plan? I can't tell."

"I don't need an entire case of torture devices when I have you right where I want you." Crouching beside her, the killer withdrew that very same knife he'd introduced to her soft tissues, setting it against her cheek, and she froze. The metal was warm despite the drop in her body temperature and the imposing elements. She could still feel flecks of her blood crusted to the blade. "You know, through all your noise and jokes and distractions, you're really just a scared little girl with no one around to protect her."

Scared? Yes. Little girl? No. Though compared to his size, she didn't blame him for making that assumption. Lila reverted into the overly upbeat persona that'd kept her from breaking apart so many times before. Her cheek pressed into the blade as she smiled. "Haven't you heard? Women are allowed to vote now. We have jobs, can choose not to have kids and fight our own battles."

His responding smile set in place as he framed her chin in his free hand. Right before the tip of the blade cut into her skin. Stinging pain ticked her heart rate higher. In a single move, he'd nearly sliced that fake smile off her face. Blood dripped down her chin and hit the cave floor. "How are you going to fight me when you're bleeding out all over the ground?"

That was a good question. One she'd have to come back to as he released her and took position standing over her. Her weight dragged her back to the hardened, rocky floor. At least this cave didn't smell like decomposition. "Just get it over with."

"Get it over with?" He cleaned the blade with his jacket. Much thicker than the long-sleeved shirt he'd worn before. Which meant he'd prepared for all kinds of weather before shoving Sarah Lantos off that cliff. "Are you really that eager to die?"

She had been once. And while that cavern of loneliness and Branch's rejection had spread to the smallest crevices of her body—clawed her into a thousand little pieces—she didn't want to die. For the first time in years, the numbness had receded, leaving her raw and exposed to the slightest stimuli. The feel of the rain on her skin, the sound of the wind roaring through the cave opening, the scent of something akin to burnt wood.

"The big villain speech. Obviously, you're not going to kill me until you've made me suffer like Sarah Lantos." Lila tested her brain's command of her fingers and toes. The blade hadn't caused enough damage to sever her connection to her limbs, but she'd sustained multiple injuries being tossed down that hill. Coupled with the bruises on her ribs, she was pretty sure she'd broken something. "That's a good place to start."

"It doesn't matter what I say. What matters is my plan for people like you. People like my sister." The killer looked down on her as though she was nothing more than a patch of mud under his shoe. "She tortured me for years, you know. In little ways at first. Pinching me under the table at dinner, adding hot sauce to my food when I wasn't looking. Her face would light up every time she got a reaction out of me, but when I told my parents, no one believed me. She had this uncanny ability to cover her tracks. She moved onto testing her skills with knives while I slept, slicing between my toes and the bottoms of my feet. Still, my parents wouldn't believe their daughter could inflict such harm. After a while she found threatening me to stay quiet by hurting my dog worked just as well as physical torture. I loved that dog more than anything, and she took it from me for fun. All while pasting a smile on her face to deflect suspicion. Much like you do."

The comparison was delusional. There was no other way to describe it. She'd never hurt an animal, let alone another person. She'd never gone out of her way to inflict pain and suffering, but to the man standing above her, she might as well have been the one to commit those unforgivable sins he'd survived.

"Sarah Lantos was…your sister." The pain in her torso intensified with every word. She wasn't sure how much blood she had lost, but she didn't have an endless supply. The longer she laid here, the sooner she'd lose her fight to escape. Lila leveraged her weight into her elbow, cataloguing her injuries from head to toe. Too many. She wanted nothing more than to sink back to the floor and lose herself in unconsciousness, but that would mean giving up. She wasn't ready to die. She'd just started to live despite the heartache that came with Branch's accusations.

"It wasn't until we were in our teens the psychologists recognized her antisocial personality disorder, but by then, the damage had already been done to me. My parents, they realized their mistake when they found me bleeding out all over the kitchen floor after I took the remote from my sister to watch my show after school one day."

Retracting one arm from his coat, the killer exposed his forearm. A thick, jagged scar trailed from his inner elbow to his wrist. The tissue hadn't healed well, much like the scar across her throat. Or maybe the damage had been beyond the physicians' capabilities. Her scar almost seemed to burn in response.

"They finally faced the monster they'd created. The way she hurt others without any kind of remorse, how she went out of her way to push their boundaries, the manipulation tactics she used to get away with her behavior. Years too late. Still, they went out of their way to get her help instead of locking her up where she belonged."

Acid churned in Lila's gut at the realization she and this killer had more in common than most. How the people who were supposed to love and care for them had betrayed them, refused to believe them, ignored their pleas for help.

But trauma didn't erase the violence he'd inflicted on his sister or her, and it sure as hell didn't justify it.

"She kept torturing me." The killer's voice lowered an octave, freezing her in place. "Drove away any woman who might show interest in me with lies of abuse and infidelity. Got me fired from multiple jobs by sleeping with my superiors. Even after my little stint in a psychiatric ward based off a false police report she filed, she set out to destroy me for no other reason than I was something in the way of her having my parents' full attention."

Lila didn't know what to say to that, what to think. She wasn't that person. But because she'd relied on a persona to bury all the bad and hide from the pain she couldn't rid herself of, he'd equated her with the nightmare of his past. She could see it now, the slight manic gleam in his eyes with what little sun broke through the storm clouds. Nothing she said would convince him he was suffering from a delusion. Not even her death. He would kill her, then he'd move onto his next target. And the next. Until the police finally caught up with him. "So you killed her."

So many innocent lives destroyed, all because no one had believed him when he'd needed it most. She couldn't help but wonder what would have happened had she not kept her pain all bottled up as Ranger Barbie but instead unleashed it on the people around her. Would she have become a killer as he had? Would she have met Branch and found her dream job? Would she still have fallen in love or let the darkness consume her?

"You think she didn't deserve to die for what she's done to me?" He was right back in her space, putting himself on her level, sliding the tip of the blade across her throat. Almost lovingly.

"I think you like listening to yourself talk." Lila pressed one palm into the ground. She could stop him. She just had to figure out how to get her body to stop bleeding. And ignore the gut-wrenching agony ripping through her heart.

The truth was, none of those questions mattered. She had buried her pain underneath layers of pink and glitter and bleach because the idea of taking it out on others as her brother-in-law had taken his domination out on her had sickened her down to the bone. She'd found the safety she'd been craving since she was seventeen years old by getting lost and finding small pieces of herself in Zion National Park. And she'd fallen in love with Branch because he'd been the first person to make an effort to understand her, broken or not. He'd taken a good long look at all the darkness she hid from the world and held her anyway. And she loved him for it. Stupid heart. "To be fair, I did ask for the villain speech, but I really don't want your voice to be the last thing I hear before I die."

Her scalp burned as he fisted a hand in her hair. "You really don't know when to keep your mouth shut, do you?"

"No." Lila brought her boot between them and slammed her heel into his groin as hard as possible. The blade nicked her skin as he fell back with a scream of agony. It bounced off the walls and drilled deep into her soul. "That's more like it."

Getting her feet under her, she fell forward toward the exit, as though her body knew exactly where to go. That sense only lasted a second before a hand wrapped around her ankle, and she hit the ground. The breath knocked out of her as she reached for the cave's entrance. It was right there. All she had to do was run.

Her vision blurred as the killer flipped her onto her back. "Let's see how loud you can scream this time."

Chapter Twenty-Six

He'd waited. And waited. But there was no sign Lila intended to meet up with the SAR team.

But while Branch was more than ready to admit she liked to disobey orders to get under Risner's skin, she wasn't stupid. She wouldn't risk her life in a storm like this to make a point, and the rangers back at headquarters hadn't seen her.

Lila was missing.

Which meant something had happened in the time he'd left her in this very spot and when he'd pulled his head out of his ass to come back and apologize for the way he'd treated her. And Branch had an idea who might've been involved.

He scanned the ground in circles, frustration building each time the rain corrupted evidence of her boot prints. The first print had been protected by an overhang, pulling him down a narrow slot canyon worn into smooth curves over the years. He'd recognized it from their two days together. The subsequent prints had washed away in the storm. Every shred of evidence, every clue telling him where she might've gone erased in a matter of minutes. He couldn't fight back the desperation that'd nearly destroyed him after the landslide.

The killer had come back to finish what he'd started. Branch didn't have proof. It was literally vanishing right in front of his eyes, but he'd always trusted his gut. He followed the slot canyon, recovering mere divots of her footprints. Until they just…stopped. She must've taken a wrong turn. Doubled back.

Crouching to get a better look at the patterns left in the mud, he tracked Lila's divots. But her prints weren't the only ones lingering. Another set had followed her in. Deeper. Harder to wash away despite the storm's relentlessness. No ridges or treads. Just impressions. Bigger than his partner's.

And right in the center of one, rivets of brown mixing with rainwater. Like slicked oil refusing to give up the fight against a more soluble opponent.

Blood.

Fire burned up Branch's throat as he shoved to stand. Lila didn't carry any weapons, which meant she'd been injured. He couldn't tell how badly, but enough for the killer to abduct her a second time. Damn it, he should've been there. He should've known the son of a bitch wouldn't let her go. Lila had tried to tell him. The killer was convinced she was just like Sarah Lantos, that she deserved to suffer for her sins, and Branch had left Lila to fight this alone because of some warped sense of protecting himself.

His blood pumped too hard. His throat raw from swallowing the growl clawing through him.

He marched straight out of the slot canyon. She wasn't here. The killer wouldn't have left her body out in the open. He'd want Lila to suffer as promised, secluding her. Branch had returned to the trail in less than thirty minutes after he'd turned his back on her and hadn't seen any evidence of anyone until Risner showed his pinched face. Which meant the killer would've taken her someplace nearby. Somewhere he could take his time but distant enough no one on the trail would hear her scream.

Branch ran through his knowledge of the area. Lila was better at this kind of thing. She was just…better.

In every way.

And he loved her.

More than he relied on his fear. More than his isolation. He loved every inch of her, complete with her shame, her secrets and unwillingness to bend. He loved her meddling and impulsiveness and the way she made decisions based solely on her mood. He loved the flares of pink on her uniform and the way she protested Risner's control by bejeweling her belt against regulations. He loved the way her body had melted into his when he'd kissed her, as though she'd always been the missing piece of his soul he'd lost in the divorce.

But he mostly loved how she'd dragged him back into the light with her unending invitations to show him around Springdale, to meet for coffee and when she'd thrown him a surprise birthday party in the break room. He still couldn't figure out how she'd learned about his birthday, but it didn't matter. She'd stood in the middle of that linoleum-coated corner of the office with balloons and a cake made just for him with that gorgeous smile on her face and daring in her eyes.

He loved her.

And he would do whatever it took to get her back.

Branch rushed from the slot canyon, taking in as much detail as his brain allowed. Rain pummeled the tracks he'd followed into the canyon, but he could still make out the increasingly rare divots she'd left behind. None of them faced the direction of the valley, wider on one end compared to the other. Had she backed up? Stumbled away after being injured?

His boot met the edge of the upper rim. And then he saw it. The drag marks about ten feet down. They were similar to those he'd found in the landslide. Scrambling to get a better look, he scrubbed water from his face. These marks were much deeper than the ones he'd come across before, and he gauged the distance between this position and the top of the rim.

She'd been…pushed. Branch scanned the surrounding area. And found another set of drag marks. Rocks and bushes acted as obstacles between the first point and the second, but there was no denying the pattern. He descended the incline and froze. Blond hair clung to the branches of a scrub brush. Her hair must've caught on the way down, ripping free from her scalp. He untangled the strand, too many images assaulting his brain as he played the scenario marked in the earth out. The killer had injured her, then pushed her down the hill.

Blood seeped in the stone there. Another cluster of hair suctioned to a prickly pear cactus a few more feet down. His heart worked overtime as the pieces of her disappearance came together. Pushing himself down the last few feet, he crouched at the base of the incline. Next to the largest impression cast in mud, where she'd landed. "What happened to you, Barbie?"

Standing, Branch circled outward from the point of her last known location until another set of tracks took shape. A smooth boot tread with a slight drag behind it. Son of a bitch. He'd taken her. But where?

He didn't have time to think of a strategy. Only time to act. But the radio was already in hand. He called through to Risner and relayed his location. He'd burned through whatever calories the oatmeal from this morning had provided. His legs ached, his energy levels had gone well beyond exhausted, but he couldn't stop. "Hang on, Lila. I'm coming."

The fear he'd given into that had driven him away from Lila had no room in his chest as it was slowly replaced with need. For her. To have her within reach. To hear that rare laugh she reserved for certain people. To absorb that inner sunshine to counter his darkness. In that moment, Branch was convinced he'd die without it. He needed her more than he needed his next breath.

Blackened tree branches clawed at his face, clothes and pack as he navigated the base of the valley, but the sting was nothing compared to the agony tearing through him at the thought of being too late. Each track in the mud he recovered was lighter than the one before it. Soon, he'd lose the trail altogether. Lose her forever.

Not an option.

Branch broke through a dense collection of trees ahead, into some kind of clearing he'd never seen before. Desert grass had overtaken the area, camouflaging evidence the killer had dragged Lila through. The trail here was a little more worn without the protection of trees keeping rain from corrupting the boot prints. There was no next step to follow. As though the killer had vanished into thin air.

In an instant, he was lost. About what to do next, where to go. Except that invisible thread that'd developed over the course of the past few days—the one tied directly to Lila—tugged harder.

He had no other choice than to follow it. He was her last resort. The only person who hadn't given up on her. The storm was only growing worse, pinning Risner and the SAR team in place. Lila's family had betrayed and shunned her when she needed them the most. Their fellow rangers wanted nothing more than to see her fail. And he...he'd turned his back on her.

That connection—however bruised and broken after what he'd said—was still there, guiding him forward. His feet were moving without conscious effort, leading him straight ahead.

A rise in the valley wall took shape to his left, and he slowed. To listen. To wait. Despite everything she'd faced, Lila Jordan was without a doubt the strongest person he'd ever met. Stronger than him. And she would figure out a way to stay alive until help arrived. He just hoped she didn't give up before then.

Grass parted as he maneuvered through the clearing. The rain lightened into a drizzle, slowing the destruction of evidence, but the damage had already been done. Mere rings of mud bled through trampled grass every so often. Branch pulled up short. The grass. Broken and bent stalks of wheat-like feathers swayed under the influence of the wind, revealing the path the killer had taken through the field.

A second burst of adrenaline filtered into his veins. She was close. He could feel it, feel that tug in the center of his chest. He didn't know how to explain it, and he didn't care what it meant, but as long as it was there, he'd follow. He'd fall to his knees for his woman. Hell, he'd crawl if she asked him to.

He'd cut himself off from everything and everyone to keep himself from getting attached to another human who could hurt him. Love had ruined him once. He'd done whatever it took to avoid it from happening again, but he'd never been a match for Lila. Not chasing it was impossible when it came to her. He wanted Lila to ruin him. Because she was worth whatever chaos she brought into his life.

The trees grew dense along the outer edge of the clearing, the grass thinner. He was on the verge of losing her again, but he wasn't about to give up. Not when everyone else had. Lila Jordan had crawled beneath his skin and carved her name with manicured nails on his heart. He was a marked man. Entirely hers.

Movement rustled through the blackened forest about a hundred yards ahead, though he couldn't make out what had disturbed the trees. Then came a dull pounding. Unsteady, hurried. Footsteps? Every cell in his body hardened with battle-ready tension. Branch ducked behind one of the larger trees. Waiting.

Then he saw it.

That flash of familiar blond hair.

Lila. She threw her attention over her shoulder, one arm clutched to her side. Her uniform had torn in places, streaked with blood and caked in mud. But he'd recognize her in the dark or completely blind.

"Lila!" Swinging himself into her path, Branch secured his arms around her middle, bringing her into his chest. Where she belonged. Hints of her scent drove into his lungs and released the vice in his chest. He could breathe easier, see clearer, think better with her here. As though the world had gone from black and white into full-blown color with her mere presence alone. That was what she'd done for him. Bought him back to life after losing all meaning. She was his meaning now. His purpose. "I've got you."

Her fist connected with his jaw, throwing his head to one side. "Let me go!"

Lightning erupted behind his eyes. Damn it all. This

woman. Tightening his arms around her, he pressed his mouth to her ear. She was in survival mode. Desperate to escape. "It's me. It's Branch. You're safe."

"No." Tears streaked down her face as she struggled to get free of his grasp. "I'll never be safe. Not from him."

"Look at me." Branch framed her chin in one hand, turning her attention to him.

Lila's eyes rolled into the back of her head. Just before she collapsed.

Chapter Twenty-Seven

She liked the dark. She could admit now that part of her had missed it.

Stab wounds tended to do that. Made you think about all your life's choices and regrets. They weren't lying when they said your entire life flashed before your eyes in your last seconds. Lila could see where she'd gone wrong. How she'd deluded herself into believing—down to her very core—that becoming someone else hadn't fixed her problem. It'd just made them worse.

She was back in her seventeen-year-old body. Sneaking into her childhood home through her unlocked window in the basement window well. Her mom wasn't home. Her dad had gone to work. Her sister and brother-in-law had moved out. And she was hurting. So much. She'd just wanted to go home, for the pain to stop. To be loved again.

She crawled through spider webs and decomposing mouse carcasses that'd gotten caught in the window well and couldn't escape, studied the very bed where she'd metaphorically died that night her brother-in-law put his hands—and other things she didn't want to think about—on her.

Her dad's pocketknife was right there in the nightstand. Right where she'd left it. Her mother must've missed it when she threw everything on the front lawn that day three weeks ago. The day Lila had been discarded as nothing more than garbage. Or maybe her mom couldn't bring herself to get rid of it. Didn't matter.

Lila knew what she had to do. It would be easy. All she had to do was pick up the knife, and everything would be okay again. She took one last look around the room, catching sight of silky blond hair beneath the bed. Getting on her knees, she got a better look. One of her Barbies, the one with its pink cowboy hat and pink jacket with fringe. The kerchief was stained with marker but was still tied around Barbie's neck no matter how many times she'd tried to take it off. She clutched the too-thin doll like a lifeline, but Barbie couldn't fix this hole inside her chest. She had to do it herself.

And set her dad's pocketknife against her throat.

A rushing filled Lila's ears. Her pulse? She was alive. Barely. But alive. The world tilted as a set of strong arms held her upright. Her vision wavered. In and out. In and out. She could've sworn she'd heard Branch's voice, but that wasn't possible. He'd left her. Just like everyone else.

Her body felt too heavy, her bones too big for her skin. Pain erupted from both sides of her ribs. Throat burning, she peeled her eyes open, and the world exploded with sensory overload. Bark bit into the back of her scalp. When had she sat down?

Movement darkened the edges of her vision. An outline materialized in front of her. Then dark eyes. The darkest brown she'd never been able to recreate in her morning coffee.

Branch's eyes.

"Lila, can you hear me?" His mouth moved, but the words sounded like they'd been put through a blender.

He was here. Or her brain was playing tricks on her. She couldn't be sure. The man whose love language was comprised of growling and glaring set his palm against her cheek. "Where are you hurt? I need to know what to focus on first."

"You're pretty." Her head became too heavy, rolling with the pattern of smooth bark at her back and into his touch. This wasn't real, though. Just a whole bunch of electric pulses her brain fired to make her final moments as pleasant as possible, and she could die in peace. How were you supposed to run from the things in your head? *Good job, brain.* But even if this wasn't real, she'd been wrong to manipulate him with fake smiles she didn't mean, forcing a surprise party he'd hated and trying to get him to open up to her.

All of it had been a lie. A halfhearted one at that. This... The pink, the death threats, the bedazzling... None of it was her.

Bleeding out in that bedroom had rewired apart of her brain that told her if her family couldn't love Lila anymore, all she had to do was become someone else. And Ranger Barbie had been born. But Branch had looked past it. Seen the real her underneath all the makeup and manicures and kerchiefs. He'd seen the unlovable Lila and run in the other direction like everyone else. She didn't even blame him, but holy hell she was tired of being someone she wasn't. And Ranger Barbie hadn't done her a damn bit of good when it'd mattered. She'd still lost the one person she wanted the most.

"You know. You were right." Why did her tongue suddenly feel like she'd licked sandpaper? "I was craving attention. I'd never done that before. Until I wanted yours."

That grizzly-bear expression softened in the smallest

relaxing of his eyes. She probably would've missed it if he wasn't a conjuring of her own mind.

His fingers threaded through her hair at the base of her skull. "No. I was wrong, Lila. The things I said to you were abhorrent and untrue. I'm sorry I pushed you away. I've taught myself to become so independent since the divorce, I refused to let anyone in. I thought I could handle it, but it's really a terrifying and empty way to live. Then you came along and blew up my whole world like a pink glitter bomb. You brought color into my life, and the only thing I could think to do was run because I was afraid of how much I'd been missing it. But, damn, woman. Trouble never looked so fine. I want you. More than anything and anyone I've wanted before. Because I love you. All of you. I love Ranger Barbie and Lila and your death threats and the whole pink nightmare. I know you lost your family, but if you give me the chance, I'll be your family now. I'll always choose you."

He pressed his forehead to hers, one hand gripped on the back of her neck. "And I'm going to get you out of here."

It was everything she wanted to hear. Her nose burned with the impending breakdown she'd scheduled after getting stabbed. "I hope you're real because if you aren't, this is a very cruel dream, and my ghost will haunt you until you die out of spite."

His hands slid to her low back and beneath her knees, and Branch hefted her against his chest. "I wouldn't have it any other way, Barbie, but if it makes you feel any better, I'm real. I'm here, and I'm not leaving you ever again."

He took a single step.

And a gunshot echoed off the surrounding cliffs.

Branch jerked forward with a grunt. His hold loosened on her frame, and she pitched forward. The ground rushed up to meet her—faster than she expected—and a scream burst free of her chest. His weight crushed her into the ground, reinvigorating the pain in her sides. But Branch wasn't moving.

Didn't even seem to breathe.

Digging her fingernails into his shoulders, Lila tried to roll him off of her. Real. He was real. He'd come for her again. And the words he'd said... He loved her. A flood of prickling warmth shot from her head to her toes at the realization her brain wasn't playing tricks on her.

But something else—something hotter and liquid—drenched her uniform shirt. Blood. No. *No, no, no.* This wasn't happening. She'd just got him back. He'd chosen her.

Struggling against the bruises and the stab wound across her torso, she rocked him back and forth. "Branch, you have to get up. We have to move. Please. I love you. I love you, too. Okay? I brought color into your life, but you brought feeling into mine. I was numb before I met you. I thought I had to be something I'm not for people to love me, but it only made things worse. I was scared of the things you made me feel because I didn't want to feel, but I don't ever want to be numb again. So you have to get up. Please."

An outline took shape, peeling away from the black trees surrounding them. The killer. He'd found them. It didn't matter how hard she'd fought to escape that dark little cave or the hollowness in her chest, he'd never let her leave this park alive.

Her hands shook as she set them on her partner's shoulders, but his eyes had slipped closed. He was losing consciousness and too much blood.

"Branch." His name broke on her lips. "Branch, get up."

"There's nowhere you can run that I won't find you, Ranger Jordan." How had the killer gotten so close without her noticing? Or had her body started shutting down? He closed in, standing above her beside Branch's unmoving frame. "My sister thought she could hide once I was released from the mental institution. She was wrong."

He took aim.

Throwing her arms over Branch, she stared at the end of the gun barrel. It took everything she had left to keep her voice even, leaning on that massive confidence Ranger Barbie had always given her. "Just finish it. If you don't, I'll dismember you so completely, the devil won't know what to do with you when you get to hell."

"Always with the jokes." The killer kept the gun steady. This was it. This was where she and Branch ended, just as they'd gotten started. Not how she pictured it in all those late-night fantasies. "You never cease to amaze me, Ranger Jordan, but you're not laughing now, are you?"

A deep warning penetrated through the small clearing where she and Branch had gone down. A blur of tan fur and fangs broke into her vision.

The killer turned the gun toward the new threat, but it was too late. Claws sank deep into the killer's chest, and he vaulted backward. His scream jerked Branch back into consciousness.

A second gunshot tore through the adrenaline-induced haze that'd taken over her body, and the mountain lion that had attacked sank to the ground.

Where had he come from? Cougars rarely attacked unless provoked. Her heart clenched at the thought of the animal sacrificing itself to save her and Branch, but she wasn't about to look a gift horse in the mouth, either.

"Lila, run." Branch's pained voice barely reached her over the hard thud of her heart. Rolling onto his back, he clamped a hand against his shoulder. Blood seeped through calloused fingers and spilled over the back of his hand. Fingers that'd held her with such care and acceptance. Now stained with blood.

Biting against the moan of pain in her throat, she slid her hands under his shoulders and pushed him upright. "I'm not going anywhere. You owe me a coffee date, and you're not getting out of it this time."

His laugh cut short as another growl broke the silence.

The killer launched himself at them.

Branch brought his knee up in time to neutralize the collision, then kicked out as the killer took aim. At Lila. His heel connected with the killer's chest and sent him spiraling backward into a tree. Then Branch was on his feet, his inhales strained and shallow. "You can't have her."

A frustrated scream tore from the killer's throat as he practically threw himself at Branch. Her partner used the attacker's momentum against him, stepping aside and planting his elbow into the killer's back.

The man who'd killed Sarah Lantos—his own sister—turned the gun on Lila, and everything inside of her went cold. "Neither can you."

He pulled the trigger.

But nothing happened.

The killer tried again. And again.

Branch didn't give him time to test it a fourth time. He scooped up a rock from the ground and swung it into the killer's head, knocking their assailant out cold. In the aftermath of adrenaline, Branch's legs failed to hold his weight, and he dropped to his knees.

But Lila was right there. Holding him upright as he'd

held her in the desert last night while she exposed all the broken pieces of herself. She swiped her thumb across his bottom lip. "Hello, Grizzly Bear."

"Hello, Barbie." He smiled at her, a genuine, full-blown smile that threatened to unravel her insides. It was the most beautiful sight she'd ever witnessed. And it was all for her. "Do me a favor. Stay with me."

"Always." She clutched his hand between both of hers. Just as Risner and the search and rescue team descended.

Chapter Twenty-Eight

Branch would not go gentle into that good night.

Okay. It wasn't that serious. The bullet wound to his shoulder hurt like hell, though. There'd been no exit wound.

Once Risner and the SAR team had found him and Lila—much to the ego inflation of the district ranger—a helicopter had been dispatched to their location. The ride itself had taken no more than a few minutes, a definite improvement over having to ascend Angel's Landing with a hole in his shoulder. He'd been swept into surgery within minutes short a pint of blood or two. When he'd asked if his day could get any worse, it'd been a rhetorical question. Not a challenge.

And Lila had kept her word after the EMTs had forced her into the trauma surgeon's hands in the Sprindale ER. Once in recovery, she'd stayed outside his surgical suite until the nurses had threatened to have her handcuffed to the bed. But true to Lila's nature, she'd promised to return with straitjackets and a referral to a mental institution for each of them if something happened to him. Seemed she was as reluctant to be apart from him and he was from her. Unfortunately, to the detriment of her own health.

Which only made him love her more.

Branch scooped another spoonful of Cherry Garcia into his mouth, taking his time sucking on the hard-as-bricks chocolate chips. His favorite part. Because once he broke through their hard shell, there was nothing but sweetness and pleasure underneath. Just like Lila. Thank heaven she'd somehow gotten her roommate to smuggle in a couple pints. He was about to throw the next cup of Jell-O he saw against the wall. Though the unending days of lying in a hospital bed were made much better by the blond beauty currently glued to the romantic comedy on TV in the bed beside him.

Bruises darkened the side of her face, a new butterfly bandage interrupted the line of smooth skin along her temple, and she'd sustained a life-threatening injury herself. While the stab wound hadn't hit anything major, she'd bled for a couple hours between facing off with the killer and the time Branch had found her in the grove of burned trees. The damage to her ribs would heal in a few weeks, but it made sitting up and walking much harder. Which she made sure to complain about as often as possible. Turned out, Lila wasn't good at staying in one place with nothing to hyperfixate on, but they would both be out of here in a couple days.

For now, he'd revel in the time they had together right here in this room.

The killer—Jeremy Lantos—was, in fact, Sarah Lantos's brother. Risner and the rest of the search and rescue team had managed to hold him until the law enforcement rangers could make an official arrest and run his fingerprints through the federal system.

Upon release from a mental institution where he'd spent the past ten years of his life, Jeremy had set out to have his revenge against the very woman who'd driven him to kill. While most of his testimony would remain between him, the Springdale PD and his attorney, it seemed Sarah Lantos had tried to destroy her brother thoroughly and completely since he'd been born. What little Branch had been privy to over the past few days, he understood Jeremy's medical records had shown broken bones, burns, bruises, strangulation attempts and more—all from the time he'd been about two years old. In the end, Sarah Lantos had done such a good job of convincing the people around her of her innocence, she'd actually made Jeremy out to be unstable. It'd only taken manipulating their parents and filing a false police report detailing an attack at the hands of her brother to have Jeremy Lantos legally committed to the institution. Repeated claims he'd been framed and wrongly committed had gone unheard for over a decade before he'd been allowed to step back into the outside world.

Only to become victim to his own delusions.

A knock sounded at the door, and Branch did his best to hide the Ben & Jerry's in case one of the nurses took it upon themselves to confiscate it. But it wasn't a nurse. Suspicion turned sweetness bitter at the back of his throat as Risner stepped inside.

"Ugh." Lila didn't need a mood ring. Her face revealed everything she was feeling, and the painkiller they had her on had stripped away any kind of filter she'd honed over the years. "What the hell do you want, dearly detested? My esteemed rival? My beloved nemesis?"

It took everything Branch had not to laugh, but since he was technically still employed by the National Park Service, he'd see how this played out.

"Now, now, Jordan, is that any way to talk to your superior?" Risner clasped his hands behind his back, taking position between their beds.

"Sorry. What the hell do you want, sir, whose presence I barely tolerate? No. That's not it. Fellow person who has improbably managed to live past the age of nine. No. I can do better. To whom it may concern, because rest assured, that person is not me. Wait. Does that work?" She tried to see the TV around the district ranger's rail-thin frame but must've overdone it. Slapping a hand over her side, she turned her face into her pillow to mutter a few favored curses.

"Stop moving. You'll tear your stitches." Branch had lost count of the number of times he'd had to remind her the pain meds didn't fix everything. She still had to rest to heal, but he also understood memories of the last time she'd been in a hospital brought back feelings of all the hopelessness she must've felt at seventeen.

"Too late." Her groan broke on a shallow whine. "Just leave me here to die. Okay? Live your life. Find new love. See Antarctica. But send me a postcard. I'll be with you in spirit."

"Are you done?" Risner watched with nothing but contempt etched into his expression. Contempt for the woman Branch loved. Strike one. "Good heavens, Jordan, what the hell happened to your neck?"

Color drained from Lila's face, and she stilled. A deer in headlights. No comeback. No death threats. His Ranger Barbie was on the verge of breaking due to the extreme stress they'd undergone during this investigation, the pain medication the doctors had her on and the attention of a man she didn't respect.

All right. Strike three. Branch's defenses snapped into

place, and he set the ice cream on the side table, brushing his hands together. "What do you want, Risner?"

The district ranger's gaze snapped to Branch, his eyes widening as though he couldn't believe an employee who'd done nothing but follow orders might not like him. It took a few seconds for Risner's little rat brain to catch up. "Murray Simpson heads the law enforcement rangers in Zion. He came to me a couple hours ago after reading through both of your statements. He'd like to make a job offer, if you'll have it."

"Not interested." Wherever Lila was, that was where Branch would go. They'd fought like hell to find each other. Battling mountain lions and killers, a landslide and the most powerful storm of the year. Not to mention their pasts. There was no way he'd ever let something as small as a job opportunity keep them apart.

"The job offer isn't for you." Risner rocked back on his heels, gaze directed at Lila. "It's for Jordan."

"Come again?" Lila's voice broke on the last word, and Branch couldn't help but lock his attention on her to gauge her reaction.

"Murray was impressed with the insights you had into the investigation, especially considering you've never had any formal training. He wants you on his team as soon as you're ready to return to the field." Ducking his chin to his chest, Risner lowered his voice. "Without you, we might not have ever figured out that Sarah Lantos was related to her killer or that she'd been stabbed before being pushed over that cliff. Due to the condition of her remains, we might have classified her death as an accident. I was wrong to assume your involvement would only complicate the investigation."

Lila pressed her palms into the mattress, pushing

herself upright, the romantic comedy on TV forgotten. "Could you say that a bit louder? I'm going to need all the other female rangers under your command to hear it."

Risner puffed his chest, a defense mechanism that did nothing except make him look ridiculous. The district ranger licked his lips. "I was wrong, and I'm sorry. Do you want the job or not?"

"Count me in." A wide smile—nothing like the fake one she'd been pasting on for everyone around her—flashed across Lila's face. It was genuine and true to the free spirit she'd locked up inside of her all these years. And, yeah, a little terrifying. But Branch would do whatever it took to make it appear as often as he could or spend the rest of his life trying. "I'd say it's been a pleasure, Risner, but I'd be lying. So I'll be filing a complaint with the park superintendent about your behavior toward the female rangers under your command. I'm sure he'll be very interested in talking with you about it. You can go."

Branch made an effort not to roll his eyes. This woman. She'd been to hell and back, but something about the smirk on her face told him she was the boss down there, too.

"Oh, wait." Lila sat a bit straighter. "What happened to the mountain lion that was shot? Is he okay?"

"The vet was able to recover the bullet without any problems. He'll recover in a few weeks, and the vet team will release him back into the wild." Risner left the hospital room with a nod as goodbye.

The second the door closed behind him, Branch was swinging his legs over the edge of the bed.

"What are you doing? You're going to hurt something." That intense blue gaze he'd happily take another bullet for centered on him, and Branch's entire world threatened to explode in vivid color all over again.

"I'm already hurting." He grabbed for his half-full pint of Cherry Garcia and hobbled to her side of the room. Then offered her the goods. "Might as well get some other benefits out of it."

She took the Ben & Jerry's and the spoon, diving right in. Her face smoothed into pure pleasure as the ice cream melted in her mouth, and suddenly he couldn't wait to get the hell out of this place and into his bed. "You know me so well."

"Apparently not well enough." He settled on the edge of her bed, no longer willing to accept the distance between them. Every cell in his body pined after every cell in hers. To the point it hurt not to touch her. To make sure this all hadn't been some screwed-up dream. Threading his free hand over the back of hers, he brought her knuckles to his mouth and pressed a kiss to the scabbed skin there. She'd fought a killer—twice—and lived to tell the tale. Was there anything this magnificent woman couldn't do? "Didn't expect you to take the job."

Her face lit up as though she'd just learned the secrets of the universe and intended to use them to her own advantage. "Do you think law enforcement rangers like pranks?"

Dread pooled in the pit of his stomach. "You cannot under any circumstances pull pranks on rangers that carry guns, Lila."

"You're no fun." Her pout didn't last long as he pressed another kiss to her wrist. Then higher at her inner elbow. Her breathing turned shallow, her pupils growing wider.

"But you still love me." He'd never felt so sure of anything in his life. The past—the divorce, the betrayal, the fear of trusting someone new—could stay where it belonged. He was ready for the future. With Lila, Ranger

Barbie and any other personalities she picked up along the way. "And you're going to be an amazing law enforcement ranger."

"Damn right I love you, Grizzly Bear." She smiled for him then. "And you love me, too."

"You got that right, Barbie." His next kiss feathered over her mouth, and he sucked in an inhale laced with cherries, chocolate and cream. His favorite combination. "Forever."

* * * * *

Harlequin® Reader Service

Enjoyed your book?

Try the perfect subscription for Romance readers and get more great books like this delivered right to your door.

See why over 10+ million readers have tried Harlequin Reader Service.

Start with a Free Welcome Collection with free books and a gift—valued over $20.

Choose any series in print or ebook.
See website for details and order today:

TryReaderService.com/subscriptions